THE CHILD ON THE TERRACE

A DANGEROUS JOURNEYS MYSTERY. VOL.4

by Virginia Winters

From The River Publishing

26 William Booth Crt.
Lindsay, Ontario, Canada
K9V 6E1

ISBN : 978-0-9959208-2-8

PRAISE FOR VIRGINIA WINTERS

No Motive for Murder

FIVE STARS "VIRGINIA WINTERS's excellent writing again enhances the adventures of her genealogist detective, Anne McPhail. While visiting relatives in Bermuda, Anne finds she's the suspect this time and moreover her own life is in danger. Can she find the real murderer in time to save herself?"

— Arline Chase, author of *Killraven, Ghost Dancer,* and the Spirit series, *Spirit of Earth, Spirit of Fire,* etc..

The Facepainter Murders

"BOOK 2 IN A GREAT SERIES, from Virginia Winters, that will thrill mystery readers and genealogists alike. Masterful writing that puts all the clues before the reader, but hides them so the ending remains a surprise."

— Arline Chase, author of *Ghost Dancer, Killraven,* and the Spirit series, *Spirit of Earth, Spirit of Fire, Spirit of Wind.*

"FOR THOSE OF US WHO LOVED *Murderous Roots,* the first volume of this detective series, let me say that the sec-ond volume, *The Facepainter Murders,* is even better. Darn it all but Virginia Winters is a master of planting hints at the end of each chapter so as to make the act of put-ting down the novel a near impossible act. I just kept reading. And reading. And enjoying the exploits of Dr. Anne McPhail and company right to the suspenseful conclusion."

— R B Fleming, historian, biographer

Murderous Roots

"FOUR STARS Recently widowed, Canadian doctor Anne McPhail takes leave to trace her genealogy. Arriving in a small Vermont town her ancestors once lived in, Anne discovers the body of the librarian she came to meet. Since the police suspect the dead woman may have been using her genealogy expertise to blackmail her clients, they ask Anne to help them reconstruct her research, uncovering several dangerous secrets before finally finding the murderer.

"An enjoyable read for genealogists as you experience Anne's elation when she finally finds the record she was searching for."
— Jane Nelson, *Amazon Reviews*

"FIVE STARS FUN BOOK, especially for a genealogist. There are many trails for the police to follow after a blackmailing librarian is murdered. The characters are interesting and the ones you think will wind up being suspects turn out to be just what they appear to be while others don't. I could not put it down."
— Mitzy Moo "Eclectic Reader" *Amazon Reviews*

"FOUR STARS A clever murder mystery with a window into Canadiana, a small town librarian feels compelled to investigate what appears to be a simple murder.... but clearly isn't. Our unlikely heroine finds herself in the midst of intrigue, danger, and of course some romance. Written with just the right amount of attention to detail and interspersed with wit and humor, this book should be entertaining for both mystery lovers and genealogy enthusiasts alike."
— J. Summers (Florida), *Amazon Reviews*

"FOUR STARS. Whoever said the life of a small-town librarian must be dull? As cadavers pile up, large sums of money change hands, deliberate "accidents" are narrowly averted and romances begin to blossom, the local police are still no wiser. It's time for an amateur genealogist to step in and help solve the mystery."
— Nancy Pratt (France), *Amazon Reviews*

Dedication

For Anne and Alan, companions on our journeys

Acknowledgements

Many Thanks

To readers Anne Simpson and Barb McFadzen for their help and encouragement.;

To Ruth E. Walker and Gwynn Scheltema, extraordinary teachers who introduced me to a community of supportive writers;

And to George, as always, for leaving me free to write.

CHAPTER 1

The Andalusian donkey is patient and strong, a very kind animal that can become attached to one person.

Day One and Two

Anne waited for a taxi to take her from the airport to a hotel in the center of old Madrid. Around her, Spanish voices mixed with English and German and many others. Strangers all. She passed her hand over a bronze, erotic statue of a woman astride a bull. Sunshine bounced from its polished surface into her eyes, bringing unexpected tears. How she wished this were a simple vacation with Thomas, instead of a trip to mend her heart and forget him and the violence he brought into her life. She signaled the next car in the line of waiting taxis and gave the driver the address in central Madrid.

After a shower and a change of clothes, she stepped from the doorway of her hotel into a maelstrom of people: tourists, police in their tiny vehicles, children and their parents, and one determined motorist who was backing out of a parking garage she'd entered in defiance of the no spaces sign.

Anne strolled down a cobblestoned city block and, beside a statue of Cortes, took in a view that included

1

Neptune's fountain in the *Plaza de Cibeles*. Her goal for the afternoon was the Prado museum and the Velazquez painting *Las Meninas*, said by many experts to be the most important painting in Europe, in part because of its influence on later artists such as Picasso. When she found it she drifted in silence around the room devoted to the artist, stunned by the immediacy of the 400-year-old works.

Later, she sat on the boulevard at a cafe across from the museum, sipping a glass of juice and enjoying the street life. A young boy ran up to her, dropped a box on her table and scuttled off. She followed his progress across the broad avenue to the central promenade. A man waiting in the shade of a Sycamore tree, passed the boy something, money she supposed, and strode away to the entrance to the Prado. His face never turned towards her, but something about his walk was familiar. She opened the box to find a glass paperweight, the interior filled with purple and yellow violets, and a note.

Meet me at your hotel at 7 p.m.

Unsigned. The child must have mistaken her for someone else, or the person who directed him had. No doubt she would be able to clear it up when whoever it was arrived.

But no one showed at her hotel at 7 p.m., or later when she drank a glass of wine and watched the locals take back *Plaza Sant' Ana* from the tourists. Children played in the makeshift playground, even though it was almost 10 p.m.. Normal for Spain, she thought.

Madrid was enduring a general strike. Helicopters buzzed overhead, flying in ominous formations of two or three, and from time to time police vehicles navigated through the crowded street. At one end of the plaza, on a makeshift stage, a band played protest songs from the sixties, in English; at the other three policemen stood, arrayed in polished boots and holstered sidearms, but not riot helmets or long guns, at ease, watching. After a time, bored, or so Anne thought, they moved on. Hawkers, emerging from the belly of the crowd, swarmed table after table, selling souvenirs and noisemakers. She returned to her hotel on the corner, with its minuscule elevator that she entered one way and exited another.

From her terrace, as large as the room itself, she listened to the music and the voices of the crowd. Later she woke from a nightmare of the room in Bermuda where she had fired at the man who tried to kill her. The plaza, quieter now, soothed her with distant voices and snatches of music and she slept again.

* * *

The next morning, she waited in the Atocha station for the AVE train that would take her south to Seville.

Alberto de Palacio Elissagne and Gustave Eiffel designed the building in a wrought-iron renewal style when it was rebuilt in 1892 after a fire. The glass and iron roof rose above a botanical garden. Anne wandered along, taken away from the bustle of the passengers thronging to the trains by the woody smell of the gardens. At one end a gentle fountain tumbled into a pool covered in green vegetation. Part of the green climbed onto the rocks and Anne realized turtles swam under the mantle of the plants. Charmed, she sat on a bench beside the garden until time to take the train.

The AVE covered the almost six hundred kilometers from Madrid to Seville in less than three hours. Only the trees and vineyards whipping by indicated the speed. Anne slept, waking as the train arrived in Seville. She stayed in a hotel close to the bus station and left the next morning for the Andalusian city of Ronda and on to Setenil where she had rented a house for two months of repair work on her emotions.

The countryside changed, revealing olive trees in plantations that climbed up steep hills, turning them a soft blue-green. Smoke from the autumn pruning lingered in the valleys. The hills became mountains and the road more perilous but the driver, one hand on the wheel, took the turns at what seemed to Anne a breakneck speed. Another, slower country bus wound its way to Setenil.

The white villages of Andalusia, carved out of mountainsides, ravaged by war, carried on a relaxed pace of life she wanted to enter, to lose herself in and heal. Setenil, inhabited since Roman times and perhaps long before, overlooked the *Rio Trajo*. The facades of the older homes hid living spaces carved from the rock itself. Seven times the Christian kings tried to wrest it from the Moors, only succeeding late in the Reconquista, the long war that took Spain back from the invaders. It was easy to see why, Anne thought, as she walked the steep hill from the bus stop to the plaza and beyond to the villa she had rented.

The owner met her at the front of a whitewashed house set into the rock.

"Welcome, Doctor McPhail." The English voices in cafes, shops and now here startled her, even though she knew many British settled in Spain when the

4

establishment of the EU passport made travel and emigration so easy.

Anne shook hands with her host, a woman who towered eight inches over her own five foot two.

"Would you like to come through?"

They stepped across a stone terrace to a blue, rough-hewn wooden door that opened into a living room wide enough for a green sofa and two cream-colored chairs grouped before the fireplace. A cavity in the side of the fireplace promised a bread oven. A window to the front and one to the right of the doorway let in light but even at noon, the interior remained darker than Anne preferred. A pot of red geraniums set on the dining table lent a peppery scent to house. All the necessary elements crammed a kitchen the size of a walk-in closet. A powder room was tucked under the staircase. One floor up, a room with a double bed opened to a minute balcony, its railing draped with more scarlet geraniums. A bathroom, complete with shower, finished the tour.

"I'm sorry there's no bath," her landlady said.

"Suits me very well," Anne said. She wanted the woman to finish the business, to leave her in this cocoon of a house, to sort out her memories and her doubts.

Alone, she divided her clothes between a white chest of drawers and an armoire. A check of the kitchen revealed a need to shop.

The owner left behind a binder full of suggestions: where to eat, where to buy food and wine, and what attractions to see. Stepping from the dark interior into the street, she waited for her eyes to adjust to the intense light reflected from the exteriors of the houses that had received their summer coat of white paint, joining them to a tradition of the villages in Andalusia which shone like beacons along the dark mountainsides.

A few steps brought her to a plaza, large enough for a terrace restaurant. A stone wall prevented a dozen tables, sheltered under an immense overhang of rock, from tumbling into the river far below. More tables clustered near the entrance to the cafe, across a narrow roadway, infrequently bothered by cars and most often, as now, used as a playground for children. When a car did appear, calls from mothers and older children scattered the younger ones to the side, like a group of boys playing hockey on a suburban Canadian street, calling "car, car" and racing to move the nets.

She ordered a glass of white wine, sat back in her chair and took her first free breath since she left Bermuda.

One of the dozen or so children, a girl perhaps five years old, with red hair tied back in a ponytail, stood watching the others. The young woman with her, not her mother, Anne thought, tossed her long dark hair and chattered with the man who sat at their table. She shooed the child away towards the other children.

The little girl sidled around the edge of a group of three others of about the same age. They stopped playing with their dolls, fell silent and watched her. She drifted away, towards Anne's table.

"Hello," said Anne. Before she could switch into Spanish, the little girl answered.

"Hello," she said in British-accented English. "What's your name?"

"My name is Anne."

"My name is...Maria Sophia."

Her minder looked around, leaped up and ran over to her, chiding her in angry Spanish for talking to strangers. At least Anne caught the word *"estranja"* and knew that meant stranger.

"I'm sorry—" Anne began, but the girl hissed, tossed her hair, grabbed Maria's hand and hauled her away.

The waiter bustled up to her table, apologizing. "I am sorry, Senora. Maria Sophia is not allowed to speak to the tourists."

"That's okay. I shouldn't have answered her but the other children wouldn't play with her."

The waiter leaned closer and lowered his voice. "They don't think she's Spanish. They think she's *Basque* and have been told not to play with her."

"What have they got against the *Basque?*"

"Some of us lost family in the terrorist attacks."

"Esti is not her mother?"

"No, no." Another couple sat down and he drifted away.

Esti was *Basque,* but the child… None of her business. Her business was to sort out her emotions and her beliefs after the episode in Bermuda. She hadn't talked to Thomas since.

CHAPTER 2

Day Three

The next morning Anne poked her head out her open living room window and decided the weather was warm enough for a tee shirt and jeans. She wound a deep pink scarf around her neck and set off through the tunnel of rock to the cafe. Her table overlooked the River Trajo and the highway on its far bank winding its precarious way to Ronda. It was an in-between hour, before the tourist bus arrived from Ronda and after the locals had gone to work or school. Another customer sat in a corner, a few tables away, reading an English newspaper. Terraces in Spain used to be full of Spanish voices, she supposed. The people at the next table were British and the one beyond that, Irish.

Maria Sophia, too young for school, skipped into the Plaza, walking beside Esti and chatting in Spanish. They sat two tables away, drinking hot chocolate. While Esti thumbed her phone, Naomi wiggled on her chair, slipped off and tiptoed over to stand beside the man with the newspaper.

"Good morning, Maria Sophia," he said.

"Good morning, Senor Caldwell."

The child said Caldwell with a British accent. But of course she did, she learned her English here, from the British who settled in Spain. Caldwell was attractive, one of those fair-haired men who never aged, the wrinkles on his tanned face perhaps testament to an outdoor life, not years.

"Here you are."

He handed Maria Sophia a coin and she dashed away into the cafe and reappeared with two pastries wrapped in a paper napkin. She returned to her table and placed one next to Esti and sat back on her chair. She shattered her pastry into many pieces, and then inspected each shard before popping it into her mouth.

Esti hugged the child and looked around and called her thanks to the man in the corner.

"Not at all."

Their breakfast done, they strolled back the way they had come.

Anne chose a pastry from the array inside. A few moments later, her table darkened as someone moved between her and the sun.

"I thought I would introduce myself," the man said. "I'm Winston Caldwell. May I join you for a moment?"

"I'm Anne McPhail. Please, sit down." She offered her hand for him to shake. He gave it a brief, impersonal squeeze and returned it to her.

"American?"

"Canadian."

"I'm British, as I suspect you know. Canadians seem quite good at distinguishing the varieties of English that end up in Setenil." He swung his long legs out, sitting with his back to the wall behind him. He took his sunglasses off to reveal light-grey eyes set wide over a short straight nose. His wide mouth formed a broad arrowhead when he smiled.

"You live here all the time?"

"Most of it, with an occasional trip back to foggy England. I was a travel writer and from time to time still visit odd spots and earn a few pounds writing for the press at home."

"I was a pediatrician, now retired."

"What brings you to Setenil?"

"I need a month of rest and peace. Do you know the little girl who was here just now?"

"Only to buy her a pastry every morning. She's a sweet little thing and the girl who minds her—"

"Esti."

"You learned her name already? Yes, Esti. She's not the best child-minder in the world. I like to keep my eye on Maria Sophia when she's outside. Esti seems bored with her job."

"Who are her parents?"

"Would you like another coffee? *Caffe latte.*"

"Yes, thank you."

Winston raised two fingers to the waiter before he answered.

"I have no idea. I've never seen her with anyone but Esti."

"Even at night. They were in the plaza last evening. How odd."

The waiter returned with their orders.

"Juanito, do you know Maria Sophia's parents?"

He said he didn't know them either and hustled back into the cafe.

"Do you think she's Spanish?"

"Quite difficult to determine as the child seems to be multilingual." He looked out over the river and drummed on the metal table with his fingers, a soft te-dum te-dum.

"Are you worried about her?" Anne said.

"Yes."

"Have you considered contacting the child welfare people?"

"Because a little red-haired girl has a *Basque* minder? They would arrest me for human rights violations."

"Oh, surely—"

"You must be careful here, Anne. You're not at home."

Anne had heard that before, in Bermuda where she had been a murder suspect, because she was a stranger. Best keep her curiosity in check. She met Winston's eyes and saw concern on his face.

"I will."

* * *

Anne wandered back towards her tiny house, stopping in a *supermercado* for house supplies, a grocer for fruits and vegetables and a butcher for some ham for her supper. Somehow, she'd get used to the Spanish style of eating, with a dinner at lunch, tapas at 6 p.m. and a light supper at 9 p.m. or 10.

She stored her purchases in the kitchen and reached for her book, a life of Caravaggio, intending to read on the terrace. The glass paperweight sat beside it on the shelf. What was that all about? Who wanted to talk to her, or was it all a mistake?

Later, she returned to the plaza and sat at a table where she could look over the whitewashed wall to the river far below. She chose a Spanish tortilla, so different from a Mexican one, and a round of toasted bread and grilled anchovies. The Spanish version of tortilla was all about the potato, thinly sliced, layered with fiery *chorizo* sausage and covered with egg, baked in a special pan and served with a hot salsa, a staple available for any meal or snack. She drank a glass of the local white wine and finished with a *fardelejos*, an almond-filled pastry. She noticed Winston and waved him over.

"Would you like to join me?" she asked.

"I'd be pleased. Do sit here. I think you'll find the view outstanding."

Anne stood at the wall, admiring the view of the craggy hills opposite, the winding road that led up and over to Ronda, and the river below, running brown with mud after the autumn rains and, if she turned just a little, the whitewashed houses of Setenil, strung along the hillside in tiers punctuated with the orange and buff and brown-streaked rock looming over the streets.

"A strange town," she said, when she sat down. Winston had taken the seat against the wall, leaving the best view for her.

"Yes. A town that evolved out of a home for cave-dwellers. Do you know its history?"

"A little. I asked a friend who works for a travel agency for a recommendation and she suggested Setenil. You said cave-dwellers. That long?"

"There is no direct evidence of that, but at *Cueva de la Pileta* west of Ronda, habitation has been tracked back more than 25,000 years. It's likely people dwelt in the caves here too. The first known inhabitants were Roman, in the 1st century CE. The Moors occupied it from the 12th century until the Reconquista when it fell in 1484 after a siege of fifteen days. You brought your need for rest to this out-of-the-way place?"

"I had a…difficult experience in Bermuda recently. A murder happened in front of me."

"Ghastly for you." He swept his eyes around the plaza. Was he watching for someone?

"The worst was after, when a young woman detective decided I was the murderer."

"Then what happened?" He swung his eyes back to her face, caught her gaze and held it.

"Eventually, I was cleared and the real murderer caught, but not before he tried to kill me and my family. And I learned something… disturbing about myself and the man I was involved with."

"So you're here to rediscover yourself, uncover another layer of truth?"

"Perhaps. Your little girl's here," she said, tilting her head towards the entrance to the plaza. Maria Sophia held Esti's hand and kept her gaze on the ground.

Maria Sophia ran over to Winston. Her eyes were puffy and the tracks of tears stained her face. He put out his arm and she cuddled for a brief moment until at an outraged call from Esti, she plodded, head down, back to the table where her minder sat.

"She's comfortable with you."

"Yes, I think I remind her of someone, a grandfather, perhaps."

"Even though you speak English to her."

"Even though."

Maria Sophia was in a bad mood, saying no to all the offers of food, until Esti chose something for her. When it came she refused to eat it. Esti called the waiter to take it away, but the child cried and screamed and said she was hungry in several different languages. English and Spanish and some words that Anne didn't recognize.

"Of all the odd things about them, that's the oddest," he said.

"What? I don't know what that other language was. *Basque?*"

"No, Hebrew."

"Hebrew. Perhaps we're getting closer to making the call to children's services?"

"Would you have made the call if you were at home, based on the evidence you have?"

"No, no." Reporting in Canada didn't require a courtroom level of truth, but enough medical suspicion to warrant a call. She didn't even have that.

But Anne thought about Maria Sophia all the way back to her house. She trudged along a street overhung by such a weight of rock, she hunched over lest she hit her head, although the mass hung several feet above her.

When she turned the corner, the blue door of the white cave welcomed her. She turned on all the lights and sank into a soft chair. Hebrew, she thought again. Hebrew.

Later she ate her ham and a salad of marinated vegetables. She stepped out onto her terrace to enjoy the soft night air. A shadow flickered in and out of her vision just beyond the light. A person? Or a feral cat on its lonely prowl. She went back inside and slept without dreaming about Bermuda or Thomas or gunfire.

CHAPTER 3

Day Four

The overhang of rock pressed down on Anne and she was glad to escape into the dazzling morning sun of the terrace. Winston called her over.

"Good morning. If you're a person who can't stand conversation early, please tell me and I'll sit here quietly," he said.

"No, I'm a morning person. At night I fade out and want to go to sleep with the birds."

"A new chap showed up today. He just came out of the bar."

Anne turned and swivelled back. A tall heavily-muscled man, stood at the wall overlooking the river.

"I know him, I think. Something about his back. Tell me when he turns around."

"He's walking away. Who do you think he is?"

"A man who saved my life in Bermuda."

"You are mysterious. What sort of danger were you in?"

"I stumbled into a plot to kill the US Secretary of State, the one who retired last year. The killer came after me because I interfered with his plans. Ari, an Israeli, killed him before he could shoot me. It sounds so fantastic, out loud, here in Spain, in the sunshine." Anne looked again, but the man had disappeared around a rocky outcrop.

"Too dark?"

"Yes."

"Didn't you say you were a children's doctor? How did you get involved with such a thing?"

"Genealogy."

"You can't be serious."

"Oh yes. Every time I start to do an investigation I seem to run into a homicide. That's why I came to Spain. No genealogy at all, only rest and peace and thought."

"I'd never considered genealogy a dangerous hobby."

"When you delve into the past, you never know what will crawl out from beneath the rocks."

"So Bermuda?"

"Yes. I had…"

"Yes?"

"I shot at the man, too. At least at his voice. After, I couldn't believe I tried to kill someone to save myself. Guns, violence. That wasn't me. I was in a relationship at the time and it affected that as well. I have to decide about the man. Thomas."

"If you care to talk…?"

Anne met the concerned blue eyes and wanted to share her thoughts and problems with him, but it was Thomas's secret, not hers.

"Not just yet but thank you."

"Not at all. Our little girl has arrived."

This business of sitting with one's back to the wall had its advantages, Anne thought. Best for keeping watch. Was that what he was doing? Esti sat at a table, but Maria ran over to Winston. She buried her face in his arm.

"Maria Sophia, this is my friend, Anne. Would you like to say hello to her?"

A violent shake of the child's head said no.

"Here's the euro for your pastries," Winston said. "You run in and get them."

"I'll see you later, Winston. I have to do a little shopping." Anne walked away towards her house. Today she wanted to explore more of the village, but when she rounded the corner, the dark bulk of a man stood in her doorway. She hesitated. Had he been inside? After a moment, she moved close enough to recognize him.

"Good morning, Anne."

"Ari."

"We best go inside."

Anne waved Ari towards a chair. She opened the drapes, letting the morning sun in to bounce off the whitewashed walls and the mirror over the fireplace. She sat opposite.

After a few moments of silence, she asked, "Why are you here?"

"I need your help."

So payback time. Ari saved her life in Bermuda and now he wanted something.

The blonde Israeli stretched his long legs halfway across the living room, watching.

"Are you sick?" she said.

"Sick? No. Why do you ask if I'm sick?"

"I'm competent to give medical help. Otherwise, you need to go."

"Thomas said you felt you were under an obligation to me." His English was colored with the same British undertone Maria's had.

"Did you send me a note in Madrid?"

17

"Yes. I wanted to talk to you before you got here and met the child, but I had to leave. Someone thought they were moving her. The obligation?"

"You're right, but there are many ways to discharge an obligation."

"And I'm here to offer you one way."

Why did he have blue eyes and blond hair? Maybe he wasn't Israeli?

"Your name is Ari?"

"No, not now. Please call me Daniel."

"I'm going to have some tea. Would you like some?"

"I don't have much time."

Anne bustled around the kitchen, putting a kettle on the gas, gathering cups and sugar and milk and the miniature brown betty teapot she'd brought with her.

When she sat down again, he said, "It's about the child."

"What child?"

"Maria Sophia they call her but her name is Naomi and she was kidnapped from Israel three months ago."

"Kidnapped? Are the parents still negotiating a ransom?"

"No ransom. Political pressure. The grandfather is a minister in the government and the organization wishes him to vote according to its desires."

"A child as a pawn. Her poor parents." Anne leaned forward to look into Daniel's eyes. She needed to be sure he was telling her the truth, but how to know in a man trained to lie. "Is this true?"

"Yes. Why else would I be here?"

"When did you talk to Thomas?" The tea lay forgotten on a table between them. Anne touched the pot, found it hot enough and poured.

"I didn't."

"No?"

"No. Will you help me?"

"What do you want me to do?"

Daniel settled back into his chair, sipped his tea and contemplated her face. After a long pause, he said, "I want to take her back."

"What do you need me for?"

"Cover and help with her. You are a legitimate person with a Canadian passport and an address in Spain."

"The child will need her own passport."

"We will deal with that."

"How will you get her home to Israel?"

"Not a problem."

Anne prowled the room, moving the vase of flowers into the center of the dining table, turning on a lamp as the light faded from the room, putting the day's paper into a bin.

"Why can't you go to the *Guardia Civil?*" she asked.

"The officer in charge here is corrupt."

"Again problems with the police? Come on, Daniel. Police everywhere can't be corrupt or narrow."

"You saw what they were like on Bermuda."

"That was just one woman and she came around eventually."

"Here it's one man and he's the boss and he's being paid off. There have been alerts for Naomi for months and here she is playing in the plaza, where the Guardia go through every day. Why do you think she hasn't been identified? You must trust me, Anne, if I am to rescue Naomi."

She made a second pass through the room, adjusting

the ornaments back to their original position.

"I have to think about this, Daniel. You saved my life, and if we were talking about your life, perhaps it would be different, but this is another *Mossad* operation and I don't want to get involved."

"Think about Naomi. Think about what will happen to her after the vote. I'll come again tomorrow." He unfolded his body in one fluid movement and stood.

She held the door open, watching him duck his head a little when he entered the street with its overhang of rock.

He hadn't said what he wanted her to do, exactly.

CHAPTER 4

Day Five

In the morning, darkness drove Anne out of her villa, seeking light and air. She hesitated before entering the tunnel through the rock. The weight of stone above her hurried her along and out to the plaza. Winston sat at his usual table and stood up at her approach.

"Good morning."

"Good morning."

"Is something the matter?" he asked, when she sat.

"I'm…troubled this morning. A man visited me yesterday and we talked about what happened to me in Bermuda, being falsely suspected of murder. He suggested to me the police here, or at least the man at the top is corrupt. Who is he?" How perceptive he was, and how kind to notice she was upset.

"Does it matter? You have nothing to do with them."

"It matters to me. I won't feel safe here, if it's true."

"I know who he is, but nothing about his morals." Winston leaned back in his chair, folded his arms and frowned.

"Would you point him out to me?"

"I've never seen him here. He must frequent some other terrace nearer to the post."

"Where is the office?" Anne leaned towards Winston, trying to catch his eyes but he kept them averted, gazing out across the river.

"Anne, surely this is excessive? What do you want to do? Approach him and ask if he is corrupt?"

"No, I want to know who he is. Don't I need to register with them or something?"

"I suppose, if you aren't an EU citizen but didn't your landlady— "

"I have no idea. She copied the details from my passport—"

"It's a long walk up." He sat forward, jolting the table. "Up?"

"Up the hill, on *Calle San Sebastian*."

They walked along the river. By the time they arrived at the *Puesto of* the *Guardia Civil* it was after 2 p.m. and a lone officer sat at the desk.

Winston asked him the rules about passports in Spain and he checked his database. Anne's information had been submitted by her landlady and all seemed to be in order. Hopeless, Anne thought. They wouldn't be able to identify the boss this way.

The outer door opened and three men entered, all in the distinctive green and brown uniform of the Guardia. The desk officer stood and saluted. Only one officer responded, an older man of medium height. His gaze played over them, lingering on Anne. He stopped at the desk, asked a question in rapid Spanish, nodded at the answer and strode into the corner office.

"We can go," Winston said, and ushered Anne out the door.

"The boss?"

"Yes. I recognized him and he recognized me. I've seen him in a *bodega* where I eat dinner."

"But you still have no opinion on his morals?"

"It was dinner, not a strip show."

"Perhaps I should go back and talk to him."

"About what? Suspicion and gossip?"

They walked in silence back to the terrace.

Esti and Maria Sophia sat at a table with a young man. Esti tossed her long dark hair and reached out to touch his hand. He raised her hand to his mouth and kissed it. The little girl kicked the table leg until Esti spoke to her and she slipped off her chair and ran over to Winston. The young man laughed, his white teeth brilliant against his tanned skin.

"Hello, Maria Sophia. Who's Esti's friend?"

The little girl glanced back at the table and then at Anne. She leaned close to Winston and whispered.

"Would you like a treat," he asked. At her rapid nods, he gave her a euro and she skipped away into the cafe.

"What's his name?"

"Sergio."

"I wonder how he fits into all this."

"There is no this, other than what your mysterious and less-than-reliable friend told you."

"Why do you call him less-than-reliable? And he's not my friend."

"Maria-Sophia doesn't look like a captive to me."

"She's only four or five and she's been away from her family for months. Children adapt."

"Perhaps."

"I think I should call protective services."

"You'll find yourself arrested if you mention the words terrorism or *Basque.*"

"Seriously?"

"Yes."

"Thanks for taking me to the Guardia." She pushed away from the table and stood, holding her hand out. He gave it a lingering squeeze. She freed her hand and picked up her bag

"My pleasure," he said.

Anne strolled back to her villa with the memory of his strong fingers engulfing hers. He was an attractive man, even if he didn't agree with her, and not involved in shadowy organizations.

* * *

Back in her villa, Anne took out her laptop and started a careful search of the laws of Spain and the EU with regard to hate crimes and slander. A web site in English made it clear defamation was a criminal act. If she said anything, especially if Esti were *Basque,* she would be in trouble. There might be more leeway under the Child Protection laws. Canadian law required doctors to advise the authorities if child neglect or abuse was suspected but she couldn't find an equivalent Spanish law. Naomi wasn't being abused or neglected and all Anne had was Daniel and suspicion.

She heard a knock at her door and then it opened.

Daniel pushed past her, turned and slammed the door.

"What—?"

"Why were you at the Guardia post today?"

"Were you following me?"

"Tell me. You can be outraged after telling me if I have a problem."

"No, you don't have a problem. I asked about registering my passport but the landlady all ready did that."

"Who were you with?" He leaned towards her, his six feet looming over her like the rocks outside. His face suffused with blood and a vein on his forehead dilated, coiled like a snake. She backed away from him.

"Winston Cantrell. I didn't tell him your name; I talked about my problems in Bermuda." Anne watched the color drain slowly from his face and his jaw relax. The snake on his forehead disappeared. She took a breath and then another.

"Did you tell him you think Naomi is a kidnapped child?"

"Yes, even before you arrived I worried about her. He's quite annoyed with me for even considering talking to the police." Anne edged further away from him towards the kitchen.

"Because the head man is corrupt?"

"No, because he thinks I could be arrested for slander or something because Esti is *Basque.*"

"Not likely *Basque,* and I doubt her name is Esti. Whoever's running her chose the name as a cover, to keep the locals from being too friendly."

"One local is being quite friendly."

"Who?"

"A guy called Sergio."

When she reached the kitchen, Anne took a bottle of wine from her 'fridge and poured. The bottle danced on the rim of one glass, spilling a little. She controlled her trembling hand and handed the other glass to Daniel who crowded her in the tiny space. She squeezed past him into the living room.

"What's he look like?"

"About thirty years old, dark hair, dark eyes, a biggish nose, ears that stand out a bit too much, an even, attractive face. He was sitting, so I don't know how tall he is. Muscular. I think he's the boyfriend. Lots of touching and hair tossing. Sit down, Daniel. I can't stand with my neck bent the whole time."

She sat and after closing her shutters and turning on the lights, he sat too.

He took out his phone, tapped twice and turned the face towards her.

"Him?"

"Yes. Who is he?"

"We think he's the man in charge of the operation here."

"Isn't he a little young?"

"Guys in his line of work don't live long."

Death, more death, she thought.

"I read the laws on child protection here. The EU laws are strong, and there's a number I could call."

"And they would send the Guardia with a social worker or tell her they have all ready investigated. There will be a record of her parents travelling and a letter of permission for Esti to mind her."

Anne leaned back into her chair, and took a sip of her wine. Perhaps she should ask him to go, leave her alone. But she owed him her life; at least she had to listen.

"Winston was a little suspicious of the situation at first, but once I talked about reporting, he backed off."

"Who is this Cantrell?"

"A retired or semiretired photojournalist."

"I need to check him out."

"He's a kind man who gives the child a euro now and then to buy a pastry or a pop."

"Pop?"

"A coke or Pepsi or something like that, or juice."

"Anything else, gifts, offers to take her on little outings?"

"Nothing like that. All this is in the open, in the cafe. Why did you follow me today?"

"You went the wrong way out of the cafe."

"What if I'd been going home with Winston?"

"I would have waited. I need your help with this. I can't take her, run with her and take care of her alone."

"Why don't you have a partner?" Her hand gripping the wine glass trembled again and her chest constricted. Run with her. He meant kidnap the child. She didn't owe him enough.

"We had a lot of places to look. We need someone who's got a reason to go to the cafe every day, who's known to the locals and can ask to take the child for a walk without raising any suspicion."

"Naomi won't even talk to me let alone go with me."

"Come on. You're good with children, aren't you. Make friends with her."

"So I can kidnap her away from the only person she knows?"

"We're not getting anywhere. The vote is in eleven days and we have that long to take her back. I need an answer in the morning, so we can plan. You must trust me, Anne."

"I'm done trusting."

"Without trust between us, we can't save Naomi."

With that, he was gone, pulling the door closed behind him.

CHAPTER 5

Day Six

On her way to the terrace the next morning, Anne stopped at a shop selling toys made in a village craft collective. A stuffed donkey, with an embroidered red blanket covering his grey back, caught her eye. An innocent present for a lonely child, she thought.

"I'll take this," she said, and left the store with the donkey's ears poking out of her bag.

Winston sat at their table, leaning back with his face turned to the sun and his eyes closed. When her chair scraped against the stone of the terrace, he opened his eyes and looked around the plaza.

"Good morning," he said. "What have you there?"

"I bought Maria Sophia a stuffed animal, a donkey. Do you think Esti would let me give it to her?"

"Try."

Anne walked over to Esti's table.

"Esti, my name is Anne. I'm a visitor here from Canada and I wondered if I could give Maria Sophia a gift, a stuffed toy."

Esti scowled, took the toy and squeezed the body, tugged at the eyes and the tail and said, "Yes. It seems to be safe enough. Why do you want to give her a toy?"

"The other children won't play with her."

Maria Sophia carried her pastries out of the cafe and slid them onto the table. She spied the little grey donkey in Anne's hand and put out her hand.

"Would you like this?" Anne asked.

She glanced at Esti, saw her nod, and said, *"Si, si."*

"Then it's yours," Anne said.

Maria Sophia hugged the donkey to her chest, sat on the cobblestones and chattered away in what Anne thought was Hebrew. Esti spoke to her and the little girl switched to Spanish.

"Thank you," Esti said.

"My pleasure," said Anne and walked away to join Winston.

"Success?"

"She let Maria Sophia have the donkey. Maybe she'll let me spend more than a minute or two with the child after a while."

"Are you making friends with a lonely little girl or bolstering your case for calling Child Protection?"

"Both." She was doing her best to make friends with the child, in case she needed to comply with Daniel's request.

* * *

Sergio sat down at Esti's table.

"Go play," he said to the child. "Go talk to the lady who gave you the donkey."

Maria Sophia skipped over to Anne. Sergio watched her for a moment until he saw Anne pull out a chair and the child clamber up, and then turned back to Esti.

"I need to be done with this," he said.

"Put you hand on mine," she said. "Kiss me."

"How much longer do we have to play this game?"

"Until it's over." She reached over and tugged at his ear and ran her fingers down his cheek. "We must remain in the open and unsuspected. The old man in Israel is asking for proof of life every day. Otherwise this would be simple."

"Simple? I bribed the cop. What if he takes the money but decides he wants to take us after all?"

"You said nothing about me?"

"Nothing. He thinks you are my girlfriend. But I'd rather be out of here. What about the woman over there?" He glanced over at Anne who had taken crayons from her bag and was drawing on the paper place mat for Maria Sophia.

"I heard she used to be a children's doctor. She likes kids and takes the brat off my hands for a few minutes." She tossed her dark hair and laughed and kissed Sergio on the cheek. "Don't worry so much. If I think things are getting difficult, I will rid us of the problem and we can leave."

"Rid us of the problem. You mean kill her?"

"Quiet. Yes."

"We could sell her."

"No. No. What are you thinking? Dead is better than that. And I'm getting tired of the grandfather's demands."

They stopped whispering and sat back in their chairs as a gaggle of tourists entered the plaza, laughing and talking and taking pictures. Esti called to Maria Sophia and they left.

Sell Maria Sophia the way her own best friend was sold. No. She would kill Sergio and Maria Sophia rather than let that happen.

* * *

When Esti left with the child, Anne ambled out of the plaza, following the road up into the hills that encroached on the town. Halfway up, behind a low stone wall, a pasture held three donkeys, one of them just a baby, still unsteady on its legs. They came over when she called to them and nuzzled her hand.

"You're friendly enough," she said. "I wonder if Naomi would like to meet you."

Her route took her down the hill again, past the police station and down to the center and her villa. Anne dumped her purse on the table by the door of her villa and turned to open the shutters. In the darkness a shadow of a man sat in her chair by the window. Her breath caught and she wanted to scream but no sounds came.

"It's Daniel," the shadow said.

"Why are you here? Inside my house?" Her voice cracked as her throat closed and she forced the words out.

"I need to stay out of sight."

"This is a small town. Someone will have seen you come in and soon it will be all over."

"No."

No. Not "I don't think anyone saw me". Not "What does it matter." Just no.

She strode past him into the kitchen and put the milk and fruit she carried into the fridge.

"I know who is holding Naomi," he said.

"Yes, so do I. Esti."

"No. At least not just her. We're not sure if she's just a baby-sitter or an active agent."

Anne looked across at him. No papers, no brief case, nothing. What proof could he have?

"I'm supposed to believe what you tell me?"

"What I show you."

He opened her lap top and inserted a thumb drive in the USB port. A document appeared on the screen, the heading an official US government seal.

"What's this?"

"Report from a CIA operative in Switzerland."

"The US has operatives in Switzerland?"

"Read it."

Anne sat, took her reading glasses from the drawer and started at the top. Details of past kidnappings used to extort political favors in countries from Belgium to Zambia scrolled past and then the conclusion, the who did it—names of three arms manufacturers, linked to two arms dealers, names she recognized from her experience in Bermuda. And then the details of Naomi's kidnapping. Her last name was redacted.

"Again?" she said. "Why?" Her hands curled into tight little fists.

"They foment war. You know that."

Yes, she knew that. In Bermuda it was murder and almost cost her life as well. They wouldn't stop at killing the child, once her usefulness was over. She took a breath and released her hands.

"What war? There's no war between Israel and its neighbors right now."

"Not right now, but it's always a risk, always there, beneath the surface. The more the settlements expand, the more angry the Palestinians become, the more heated the discussion in Israel, the more the Defence department buys. There will be a vote on expansion."

"So to change one vote, they—"

"Not one vote. He is very influential, the grandfather,

very important. We have to rescue her, Anne. Will you help me?" He leaned towards her, his blue eyes searching her face for the answer he wanted.

So here it was. She had to decide. Not a shady CIA operation but saving a child's life. But could she trust that all this was true? What other reason would he have to take the child? She looked away.

"I have to think about it, satisfy myself that you have the right child. I need to know who the parents are, who the grandfather is and what his position is."

"You know that I can't tell you that."

"I can't begin to consider helping you if I don't know that." She confronted his eyes again. This time he averted his gaze.

"I can't tell you without authorization."

"Are you authorized to recruit me?"

Daniel stood up and reached for the door handle.

"Her last name is Shapiro. That's all I can tell you."

"I need some time to think and decide."

"Don't think too long. The vote is coming and her usefulness to them will be over. I'll be back to ask you again." A moment later the door opened again. "Don't let Esti know your last name," he said. "I don't want her to tell them who you are."

Anne huddled in her chair until the light had disappeared from the crack in the shutters and the evening chill crept into her. She shivered and got up to make some tea. Kidnapping. How could she?

* * *

Later in the afternoon, Esti opened the heavy oak door of the town house the cartel rented in the names of Maria Sophia's fictitious parents. The scarlet geraniums drooped in the flower box below the barred ground floor window. The bars bothered her, reminding her of the house she lived in after her parents died.

"Come on, Maria Sophia. You and your donkey play outside."

From the front door, past a living room with a beamed ceiling, an archway opened into the kitchen and beyond, a door onto the patio. Patio, she thought. It didn't compare to the wide terrace behind her home in Lekeitio, in the Pais Vasco, overlooking the sea and never hot and oppressive like this place. How she hated Setenil and its rock and its hoards of tourists wandering the streets.

She shooed Maria Sophia out to the patio closed at one end by the door into the house and at the other by a wall of rock. Pots of flowers glowed against blue tiles. A basket overflowed with toys.

"Can I play inside?"

"No, you need the fresh air."

She heard a knock at the door and then two more. Sergio.

"Come in; come in."

He pushed past her, his dark eyes searching the space. "Where is she?"

His voice sounded full of fear, as though the child were an armed man waiting for him. What was he afraid of?

"On the terrace. What do you want?"

He said nothing but walked to the door, peered out at the child and returned to the living room.

"Did you phone Colette?"

"Not today. What's the matter?"

"The Guardia commander is asking for more money."

"Why? What did you tell him?"

"Nothing. Maybe the old man in Israel told the cops."

"Idiot. He was trying that on and you fell for it. We have good papers for the child and a phone number he can call to talk to the parents. He's well paid to keep his mouth shut and protect our operation."

"I told him I'd bring him some cash."

"You what?" Without a thought she brought her hand up and hit his face, his skin gave under her fingers but he caught her wrist and twisted, shooting pain up her arm.

"Otherwise he said he would arrest us this afternoon." He tossed her away, onto the sofa and sat across from her.

"This afternoon? How much does he want?" He'd never touched her before. She'd likely need to kill him before this was over.

"One thousand euros."

"They are not going to be happy with you or me. Idiot."

"We could leave."

"And have every cop in Spain after us."

"An accident?"

"And that would be all over the news. No."

She ran up the stairs to her bedroom, retrieved the money from her cache behind a stone in the wall and came back down.

"Here," she said, handing him an envelope. "If he asks for more, tell him it will take a few days."

"What about selling her?"

When she chose Maria Sophia for the child's name, she was thinking of her long-dead friend, driven to suicide by a father who sold pornographic videos of her. She would kill the child herself to prevent it happening to her, too.

"No. What kind of monster are you?"

He towered over her. "The kind that needs money. Have you thought of after, when she's no use to them anymore? What are you going to do?"

"Not that."

After he left, she stood at the door to the terrace, watching Naomi play with her little donkey, giving her dolls rides up and down the slate floor of the narrow space. What should she do with her? There were convents still in Spain. Perhaps she could leave her at one of those.

Esti called Maria Sophia and put her in her bed.

"But I'm not tired, Esti."

"It is time for your nap. Be quiet."

What was she going to do? The grandfather in Israel wanted proof of life and she sent the pictures with the newspaper daily but how much longer could they live here without becoming part of the community. People were talking to the child, especially the new tourist, Anne. She needed to call.

In Switzerland, a woman picked up the phone.

"Yes."

"Esti."

"And?"

"Some problems. Sergio is getting restless. We have been too accommodating to the Israeli with his proof of life. We should deny him his daily picture and demand a commitment."

"You do not know the Israelis. As soon as he thinks his granddaughter is dead, his vote will not be ours."

"Other parents and grandparents—"

"It is rare for the Israelis even to negotiate this far. Do your job."

"We should move her. The Guardia officer we bribed wanted more money today."

"Unfortunate. Perhaps the Guardia officer should have a fatal accident. I shall check."

"Kill a Guardia officer. That's crazy. They'll be all over every stranger in town, including Sergio and he's getting anxious. Find out what they think about denying proof of life."

"Call tomorrow. They will decide by then. In the meantime, protect the child from Sergio if necessary."

Protect the child from Sergio. Colette didn't understand that Sergio wasn't going to kill the child. Tomorrow. What if they wanted them to kill the Guardia commander? A mistake, but if they didn't follow orders others would come.

Chapter 6

The next morning Anne sat in the plaza, enjoying the sunshine flooding the terrace and the hills across the river. The rains in the mountains had swollen the dark brown water of the river far below. The rich aroma of espresso drifted from the cafe, mixed with the scent of baking. Apricot, she thought, and cinnamon. Winston hadn't arrived but when Esti and Maria Sophia came the little girl ran across the plaza, hugging her donkey to her chest.

"Thank you for my donkey," she said.

"You're welcome. Did you give her a name yet?"

"She has a secret name."

"I have one of those names—Elizabeth. Do you too?"

"Yes." The little girl leaned forward and whispered in Anne's ear. "Her name is Datna."

"That's a lovely name. What is your secret name?"

"Naomi, but I'm not supposed to tell."

"I won't tell anyone," Anne whispered. Aloud she said, "I think Esti wants you."

Anne walked back with her.

"Esti," she said, "I'm going to Ronda next week on the bus to do a little shopping. Would you and Maria Sophia like to come with me?"

38

"Why?"

"I haven't explored Ronda. Or I could take Maria Sophia if you wanted to do something else here."

"No, thank you. Her parents are away for three months and I'm not allowed to take her anywhere or even send her to school while they are gone."

"Can you call them?"

"No. They left for America two months ago and I'm only to call for medical emergencies."

"That's too bad, but I'm glad they'll be back soon."

"One more month."

One more month. Daniel said one more week. One week until the vote. If Daniel was telling the truth, and she thought he was, would Esti and Sergio release Naomi? Or would they take her away and kill her? She couldn't let that happen.

Winston arrived with his paper and sat down opposite her.

"I asked Esti if I could take Maria Sophia to Ronda, with or without her, but she said no."

"What did you expect?"

"That, but I wanted to be sure. She has orders for everything, it seems."

"Let it go, Anne. They come here every day. If one day they don't, go to the police, make your calls. Otherwise, you'll be seen as an interfering tourist who thinks she knows more than the Spanish. Remember that Forster novel, *A Passage to India?*"

"A tourist who overreacted and didn't understand local culture and customs."

"And caused a tragedy. Yes."

"Is that how you see me, too?"

"No, but—"

"I must go."

Anne rushed off towards the tunnel, aghast at tears that threatened to embarrass her in front of Winston. He hadn't met Daniel, seen his evidence, so how could he see her otherwise than a tourist who just didn't get it. Why did what he thought matter so much? She'd only known him for one week.

At her villa, she sank into a chair and waited for some of the emotion to drain away. After, she busied herself in chores.

Anne wandered upstairs to assess when she had to do laundry, back downstairs to move chairs and then move them back again. The kettle whistled and sputtered and she ran to take it off and fill the teapot. She sat in the living room to wait for her tea to steep. What was she going to do? She had told Daniel that she had to satisfy herself that Naomi was the child he was looking for. How did she expect to do that? By the time she poured her tea, she'd decided to call Thomas.

She listened to the ringing, so close she felt he could walk in her door.

"Anne? Are you all right?" His voice, so full of concern and love. Why had he lied to her and damaged what they had together? She took a deep breath to steady herself before she answered.

"Anne?"

"Yes, yes. I need some help, though. You remember the man on the plane from Bermuda, the one you said you owed one to."

"No names, I take it. Yes, I remember."

"He wants me to help him take back an Israeli child, a kidnapped child who is being held to pressure the grandfather for a political favor."

"What the hell is he thinking? You're not an operative. Come home, Anne. Don't get tangled in one of his messes."

"What do you mean 'one of his messes'?" Anne paced the room, stopping to look at the rain turning the street outside into a creek.

"His ops are always way outside normal channels. Please, come home."

"But the child." His ops. What a casual use of jargon.

"If it's true, he'll do it without you."

"He says he can't care for her on the road. That's what he wants me for."

"And when they come after him?"

"I don't know, Thomas. I don't want to leave the child if she really has been kidnapped. And I need you to get some information for me."

"What information?"

"I want to know if a couple arrived in the US two months ago from Setenil or Cadiz province in Spain with a projected stay of three months."

"I can try. If I find them, will you come home?"

"At least I won't take any unexpected trips."

"I'll call you tomorrow, noon, your time."

"All right."

"Anne. Is there still— "

"Don't ask me yet. Please."

"I'll call you tomorrow."

She sat so long, holding the phone and remembering the sound of his voice, hearing the concern, that her tea turned cold and bitter. She poured it down the sink, opened her laptop and began a search for the parents and grandparents of Naomi Shapiro. First, she assumed that this child's grandfather sat in the Israeli cabinet but there was no Shapiro listed amongst the names.

So a daughter's child. That meant she had to look deeper, at newspaper archives and perhaps lists of immigrants to Israel after the war. Shapiro was a common enough name but if the bride's father was a politician, likely her wedding was news. She began with a simple search on the child's name, looking for a birth announcement. She found one, listing the mother and grandparents. When she input the maternal grandfather's name, she got a hit on a newspaper web site that listed him as a member of the Security cabinet, the executive branch of the government. Could it be that easy? Anne double-checked her information, looking for a wedding announcement or newspaper story about the grandfather that might list his children, but nothing.

What would she be doing if her grandchild were missing? Would she go to work, attend social events and major meetings? She found a record of the apparent grandfather attending a meeting in Switzerland. But, she thought, that is what someone in his position would have to do. If he was negotiating, he had to keep this major weakness to himself.

She hadn't found much, but enough to convince her that the child on the terrace, if her name was Naomi Shapiro, was the kidnapped child.

Now she had to wait for Thomas's call.

* * *

In Culver's Mills, Vermont, Thomas clicked off his phone. He could see her: the top of her head brushed his chin when he held her and he was only five nine; platinum streaked her blond hair and her blue eyes curved upwards; her nose was too short for classic beauty but she had lovely ears, tight to her head and only big enough for the diamond studs he'd given her. She always wore them.

"Lunch, Thomas?" His mother, an elegant woman whose dark eyes and high-bridged nose were echoed in her son's face, called from the dining room.

"Coming."

"I heard you say Anne. How is she?" His mother, wearing a dark blue sweater over a cream silk blouse sat at the head of the mahogany table. The crystal and silver gleamed, set off against the dark wood of the table, dressed only with linen place mats for this, a lunch with only the two of them. How formal they always were. His thoughts drifted to Anne's more casual approach to life.

"I'm not sure. I may have to go to Spain."

After lunch, he sat in the library, making a call. The autumn sun streamed in the windows, bounced off the polished cherry of the desk and reflected rainbow colors from the decanters on the side table.

"Quin? Tom."

"What's up?"

"You remember my friend in Bermuda, who helped save our butts and the Secretary's life?"

"That sounds like you need a favor."

"She does."

"So let's have it."

Thomas gave him the particulars of Anne's request, while he watched two energetic squirrels chase each other up and down the chestnut tree.

"If this guy works for that agency, why doesn't he get the information for her?"

"I don't think she trusts him. She barely trusts me."

"You don't want her to do this."

"Hell, no. But she'll make up her own mind. You know how she is."

"I think it's a bad idea but I'll get it to you."

"When?"

"Later today. Try to talk her out of it."

"Who can talk her out of anything she wants to do?"

One squirrel dropped the chestnut from his mouth, dug a tiny hole and buried it, before running up the tree again. She was as persistent as that squirrel, he thought. Spain. He reached for the phone and arranged to fly to Spain that evening.

* * *

Later that afternoon, Thomas walked out of his lawyer's office that fronted on the square in Culver's Mills, Vermont. Autumn colors dressed the trees in scarlet and yellow. Leaves heaped in piles on the ground and blew in tumbling bunches across the grass around the heroic statue of the town's founder in the middle of the square. The white spire of the Methodist church towered over the south side and the courthouse rose at the north.

When he turned to walk to his car he met Adam Davidson, the former lead detective on the police force, leaving Erin Maxwell's antique shop. They weren't married yet although they'd become engaged in Bermuda.

They shook hands and agreed it had been a while.

"Set a date yet, Adam?" Thomas said, inclining his head toward the store.

"I'm still in law school so no time to get married. How about you? Anne?"

"I heard from her today. Got a minute?"

They walked back into the shop.

"Did you forget something," Erin called from her office.

"No, Thomas and I just want to visit. We're going upstairs."

Adam and Erin lived in a loft, furnished with pieces she collected: late Victorian mahogany sideboards, an overstuffed formal sofa, and a drooping fern in a white planter. She changed the furniture most weeks to bring a fresh look to the shop below.

Thomas sat on one of the pressed-back oak chairs in the kitchen and waited while Adam made coffee.

"What's up?" Adam asked when he put a cup in front of Thomas.

"Anne's getting herself in some trouble with her curiosity and her need to help. You remember Bermuda and the guy we thought killed Blanc?"

"Yeah."

"He claims a child in the village in Spain where Anne is living is a kidnapped Israeli child and he wants Anne to help take her back."

"Who's holding the child?" Adam leaned forward, his gaze searching Thomas's face.

He may have given up the job but not the habits of the cop, Thomas thought.

"He says the same cartel."

"Trust him?"

"To be loyal to Israel. Further than that, I don't know."

"What does Anne want?"

"She wanted me to get information to help confirm the story so I called Quin."

"And?"

"Nothing yet."

"What can I do?"

"Can you access info about who entered the country when?"

"Nope. I don't have the contacts yet. Ask after I get a job at the FBI."

"Is that the plan? FBI?"

"Depends. More likely a law practice here, but I have to see how it works out, what Erin wants to do. What's next for you?"

"Go to Spain."

"Do you need me to come?"

"No, but keep your cell on."

They shook hands and Thomas left. Adam would be there if he needed him.

* * *

At home, Thomas studied a document on the economy of Spain, where he had invested, not heavily, several years before. It didn't look good for the country, especially the high youth unemployment. Something had to be done, all over the world, to get the youth working, to take up all the destructive down time and put it to use. Without work, war, a frequent solution for too many young men, would happen. Spain was a peaceful nation since the problems in *Basque* country had been, if not solved, at least not worsened. The public, random bombings had ceased. His thoughts passed from Spain to Anne.

God damn Ari or whatever his name was. As soon as he learned she was going on vacation, he thought of how he could use her.

He poured a jigger of Glenfiddich into a crystal glass and stood at the window. His mother, cleaning the bed under her prize roses, a job she refused to leave to anyone else, waved to him. He waved back but turned away when the phone rang.

"Tom?"

"What do you have?"

"Nothing. No couple from Setenil or Cadiz province entered in the last three months. Okay?"

"Hell, no. I wanted the child to be an ordinary child, being minded by a bored girl in a village in Spain, not the focus of a blackmailing operation."

"Maybe you better give me a few more details."

"Maybe not. I'll go to Spain myself."

"What will you tell—"

"I'm telling no one anything. I'm not full-time, remember. Your agency asks for my help but doesn't tell me where to go or what to do on my own time."

"Tom—"

"No. I'll let you know if I think you should be involved."

"You may need backup."

"I've arranged some, but thanks. I'll call you if it's going south, but I don't want to put Anne in the middle, more than she is."

"They play for high stakes, although this business of kidnapping a child and extortion—I don't know—sounds like a low-level mistake. You take care. I gotta run."

47

"Thanks, Quin."

Thomas took a carry-on bag from his bedroom closet, all ready to go with everything he needed, kissed his mother good-bye and left for the airport where a private plane waited to take him to New York.

CHAPTER 7

Day Eight

Sergio tucked the envelope inside his jacket. Time to meet the cop. Esti's words echoed in his head. What kind of monster was he? Was he the kind that lived off selling children? Unbidden, a childhood prayer his Irish grandmother had taught him came into his thoughts.

"From goblins and ghosties and wee little beasties, dear Lord deliver us." Had he become a beastie?

His grandmother. All her talk about God and the Church and nothing saved her. He shook off the memories and continued down the hill to the plaza near the Guardia office. Too near.

At the plaza he stood for a moment, looking for any of the cop's men. But the commander seemed to be alone, sitting with his back to the wall at a table near the door to the bar.

"Did you bring it?" he asked when Sergio slid into the seat opposite.

"Yes, but that's all."

"I'll let you know when I need more. Expenses." The commander ran his tongue over his lips.

"You told others?" Greedy bastard. Expenses.

"No, no. But if anyone gets suspicious, I'll have to

pay him off. You understand, it's not a little thing you're asking me to do."

"All I'm asking you to do is leave us alone."

"After all, the child is kidnapped."

"So you say. The child has documents."

"No doubt forged."

"Then arrest us or take the money."

Sergio slid the envelope across the table. The other man run his tongue over his lips again, glanced around the terrace, and tucked the envelope under the place mat.

"Go," he said.

Sergio strode back the way he had come, but paused to look back. The commander thumbed through the contents. He hoped the bosses wanted him out of the way. It would be a pleasure to arrange an accident.

* * *

Anne awoke early that morning, before the sun penetrated beneath the rock overhanging her villa. The lamps, creating weak pools of light, turned the room beyond into a dark cavern. Too much gloom. She grabbed her bag and walked out and up towards the sun.

She took the route she and Winston had when they went to the Guardia detachment, and soon she passed the green-fronted building with its single patrol car parked outside. Winston told her the officers and their families lived in the building surrounding the office. The road overlooked the river and the town below. She took the opposite side and continued up, past the last whitewashed houses with lines of clothes waving in the soft wind, to where the vineyards and pastures of the neighboring farms began. The three grey donkeys and a foal watched her from behind the stone wall. It was difficult to tell which was the mother until the foal wanted breakfast and nuzzled one of the jennies. All three guarded the baby, edging her away from the stone wall when she tried to come up to Anne.

Even the donkeys knew it took more than one adult to save a child. She turned back, following the same road down into the village.

The overhanging rock turned the streets into sunless tunnels. When one opened into a plaza washed in the morning light, she sat at a table under a blue umbrella and ordered a *cafe con leche* and one of Setenil's pastries.

The pastry, flaky and delicious with butter and orange filling, arrived as the Guardia commander marched into the plaza. How arrogant he looks, Anne thought, taking in the high-bridged nose and the brow that echoed the rocky overhangs. He took a chair against the wall at a table with a view of all the others and the entrances to the plaza, but a tall potted plant, a schefflera, shielded her from his view. Soon the other tables filled with local shopkeepers, who turned their signs to *cerrado*, and met their friends at the cafes. The few tourists who penetrated this far into the village took pictures of each other sitting under the rocky protuberance above.

Anne concentrated on her pastry until another man sat at the commander's table. Anne asked the waiter for a newspaper and sat, trying to decipher the headlines with her limited Spanish vocabulary. She glanced at the policeman. His companion slid something across the table to the commander.

Something white. The man stood up, and turned his face her way. She concentrated on her paper but she recognized the face. Sergio. Now she had a link between the commander and whatever was going on with Maria Sophia or Naomi or whoever she was.

The commander peered into the envelope. His lips moved and he thumbed the contents. A bribe or a payoff. Her mouth dried and her heart raced when he stood up and walked towards her, but he passed her by. Had either of them seen her, recognized her?

The route back to her villa avoided the Guardia office. She closed her door behind her and sank to the floor. Was she going to do this? It was almost 1 p.m.. Thomas would be calling. Perhaps the parents had been located and it was all a mistake. She could tell Daniel he had the wrong child and he would leave her alone to mend her life. Her life. As soon as she had a problem she was on the phone to Thomas. He wanted an answer from her, some assurance they would be together again. He hadn't actually lied to her. He'd kept an important part of his life from her but perhaps he needed to, to protect her but here she was, pulled into his shadow world again.

A rapid tattoo at her door sent her heart into her throat and she struggled to get to her feet.

"Who is it?"

"Daniel."

He slammed the door behind him.

"What are you doing—"

"What's wrong with you? Are you sick?"

"Why—"

"You're pale and your hands are shaking. Sit down."

"You frightened me."

"I knocked at your door." He settled her into a chair, took a bottle of white wine from the fridge and filled a glass.

"I thought you were the Guardia."

"Drink."

He held the glass out to her and she sipped, shuddered as the cold wine hit her throat, and drank again. She told him about the cafe.

"So you think it was money?"

"You know the way people look when they're counting—concentrated. He was even moving his lips."

"A bribe."

"What else. Why are you here in the middle of the day?" Anne lay back in her chair and covered her eyes with her arm.

"We intercepted a message between Naomi's grandfather and the kidnappers. The cartel is demanding the grandfather make up his mind."

"Did he respond?" He sounded like he was telling her the truth. Why else would he be here?

"He's asking for proof of life. Bargaining with these people doesn't work. We have to get her out of here so they can't give him their proof."

"What if they trump up charges against me? It won't take them long to identify me and then what?" She sat forward and searched Daniel's face.

"You'll be in France. If you're arrested, when I take the child to safety, I'll come for you."

"That will only help if the charges relate to kidnapping. But they won't be. It'll be fraud or damage here or theft or something."

"They will kill her."

"I don't think I'm brave enough to do this." She stood up and paced the room.

"Anne—"

"I don't think I can. Maybe you have the wrong child and I'd be in jail for nothing."

"You won't be in jail—"

"Or dead. You'd better go. I need to think and Thomas will be calling me."

"I could talk to him."

"No. Go."

He left, closing the door softly behind him.

The phone rang. Tears stung in her eyes at the sound of his voice.

"Anne, I've called our friend in the agency to get information for me. I should have it by tomorrow, if you still want it."

She forced her words out past a lump in her throat. "Yes, I do. I saw money passed to a police official today, or at least I think I did."

"Have you decided what you are going to do?"

"No."

"And about us?"

"We're talking again, Thomas. Give me a little more time."

"I'll call tomorrow."

Anne held the phone for long minutes after he was gone. Us. Was there still an "us"?

Later in the afternoon, she sat in the plaza, her face turned to the warmth of the late day sun and watching the children play. Esti and Sergio sat at another table. Sergio spoke to Maria Sophia who skirted the other children to come to Anne.

"What's the matter, Maria Sophia?"

"They told me to come here to play."

"Good. Climb up on that chair and we'll color."

Anne had a small box of crayons in her bag, leftovers from a visit to a friend's grandchildren. She pulled them out and sketched a scene with donkeys on the place mat.

"Now you have a picture to color. Which crayon do you want to start with?"

"The red one."

While the child played, Anne looked over at Esti and Sergio. Esti was touching and kissing, but Sergio leaned away from her caresses. Trouble in paradise, Anne thought, and turned back to Naomi.

"They're fighting," Maria Sophia said. "They fight all the time about me."

"No. Grown-ups may sound like they're fighting about children but they're not. Kids can't change what adults do."

"Sergio doesn't like me."

"Do you like him?"

"No, he's mean."

Another reason to get her out of here, Anne thought, and hugged Naomi. The child laid her head on Anne's shoulder for a brief moment and then straightened up with a quick glance towards Esti.

Fearful, Anne thought. She'd have to decide soon.

* * *

Daniel drove from Setenil towards Olvera, to the whitewashed villa he rented in Torre Alhaquime. On the border between Muslim and Christian areas of Spain, the village changed hands many times during the Reconquista. On trips to North Africa he passed through Berber villages of similar design.

He parked in the rear, out of sight of curious passersby. Inside, he opened the shutters and windows, letting the air, filled with the scent of olive branches burning after the fall pruning, flood the room.

His secure phone, hidden inside the chimney flue, beeped. Only the boss, not his parents nor his lover Shoshana had the number.

"Yes," he said.

"The list may have been compromised."

"When will you know?"

"It may take some time."

"The operation?"

"As soon as you can."

Daniel returned the phone to its hiding spot, and took another from his pocket. This one, anonymous, replaced often, linked him to Shoshana. He hit call.

"Daniel."

"Yes. I miss you."

"And I, you. When will you be home?"

"A week, ten days, not longer. I'm coming to stay, my love. I resigned today." Somewhere in the moments between talking to his boss and calling her, his heart had decided. He was going home.

"Oh, Daniel." He could hear the tears in her voice, the joy. He'd promised. Now he must save Naomi and go home. Alive.

CHAPTER 8

Day Nine

Anne woke several times to consider Daniel's last words and slept again. In the morning, the house was in darkness. Opening the shutters let in little more light than had seeped around the cracks and the two lamps didn't help. Rain as loud as hail pounded the stones outside her villa. She set the Bialetti espresso maker on the burner and toasted a slice of bread.

What if they put a warrant out for her, charging her with kidnapping? Would Daniel and his *Mossad* bosses testify for her? Not likely. Would they work behind the scenes for her release, to prevent an international incident? More likely.

What if that corrupt cop charged her with something else, identity theft or fraud, or something equally difficult to refute?

The toast lay unwanted on the table and the coffee spluttered over the stove. She wiped up the mess and poured a cup. The phone rang.

"Anne?"

"Thomas. Did you find them?"

"No one of that description entered the USA in the last 6 months, not from Setenil and not from Cadiz. I asked Quin to check his sources and nothing. I think Daniel told you the truth but I want you to stay out. He can do this without you."

"He thinks it would be better if I were along. I owe him. You know that."

"I owe him, not you, not at the risk of prison."

"He saved me from prison and saved my life. What about Naomi? I can't refuse to help, Thomas. I can't."

"Will you call me?"

"If I can. It may not be safe once we're away from Setenil."

"So you decided?"

"I think so. Daniel will come soon and I'll tell him one way or the other."

"Be safe."

She clicked off her phone.

An hour later, a knock came on the door. Daniel slipped inside when she opened it.

"Did you make a decision?" He sat in the chair near the window, his eyes focussed on the street beyond.

"Yes. I'll help you. Thomas called to tell me no couple from Setenil or Cadiz province entered the USA in the last six months for a long stay. How are we going to do this?" Anne sank into the only other chair in the room and leaned forward. She clenched her hands but relaxed them a little when she saw her knuckles turn white.

"Do you think Esti will let you take Naomi for a walk?"

"Yes, I think so. I'll tell her we're going to visit the donkeys. I think she would like an hour without Naomi and I think she trusts me to bring her back."

"Now?"

"We've missed their morning visit. They usually come back about 2 p.m. for lunch and go home for siesta. If Sergio is with them, it'll be easier because they are still flirting, whether or not it's real."

"I'll meet you on the road near the donkey pasture. Don't get in the car if you're not alone or if cars are coming. Don't keep looking around for me. Give me fifteen minutes and if I don't show, take her back to the cafe." He turned from the window to look at her.

"Why wouldn't you come?" Did he think he was suspected? Would he tell her? Anne stood up and paced the room, ten steps one way, eight the other, back and forth.

"Always have an alternate plan, Anne. Always a plan B. Sit down. If anyone were watching—"

"Is someone suspicious?" She walked into the kitchen and put her kettle on the stove.

"No. How well do you know Winston?"

Winston. What did he have to do with this?

"I met him when we came here."

"So not a resource?"

"No. I have no one here, Daniel. No one, if our plan goes south, if you are hurt or dead or choose to abandon me."

"I won't abandon you. A woman in Italy, off the grid, a resource of my own, will help you if anything happens to me."

"Italy. You didn't say anything about Italy."

"Don't worry about Italy. First we're going to Barcelona."

"So this afternoon, at the donkey pasture?"

"Yes."

Anne slumped in her chair, drawing her arms to

her chest. Her heart raced, her chest tightened and the room grew distant and if Daniel spoke, she heard nothing. At the donkey pasture at 2 p.m..

CHAPTER 9

By 1:45 p.m., Anne sat at Winston's table, picking at a plate of ham and olives.

"Something wrong?" Winston asked.

"Nothing. I'm glad the rain stopped because I want to go for a walk this afternoon. Do you think Esti would let Maria Sophia come with me?"

"Sergio's waiting for her. She might."

Anne swivelled her head towards the door to the cafe. Sergio sat at Esti's usual table, alternating between looking at his watch and the entrance of the street into the plaza.

"Tell me when they get here, would you?"

"Yes."

A newspaper lay on the table in front of Winston.

"What's the news today," Anne asked.

"More demonstrations in Barcelona and Madrid because of the unemployment and austerity."

"I think all this austerity is breaking the backs of the poor. I thought the way to mend a consumer society was to put more money in the hands of more people."

"Inflation."

"I suppose. The Canadian economy withstood the recession well, but we went through this austerity exercise years before."

"I wish Britain had." He drummed his fingers to a rhythm only he could hear.

"Is that why you live in Spain?"

"No. Not the money but the weather... Your retirement is well-funded?"

"I inherited money from a great-aunt I never even knew. That's what started my interest in genealogy. I wondered who else was out there that the family never spoke about."

"Did you find anyone?" He cocked his head a fraction. "They're having their lunch now."

"Not alive. The aboriginal fifth great-grandmother was a surprise, to me, if not my mother. I think she suspected some such thing. Let me know when they finish. What are Esti and Sergio doing?"

"Playing footsie under the table. How do you begin?"

"The search?"

"Yes. I've never even tried."

"Ask questions of every family member you can find, especially the elderly ones. Join Ancestry.uk and put in your name or your father's name and follow the trail. There are lots of UK resources. The British seem to be genealogy-mad."

"I think you should ask now. Maria Sophia's wiggling."

Anne strolled across the plaza to Esti's table.

"Hi, Esti."

"Good afternoon." Anne supposed Esti couldn't help but look haughty, with her high-bridged Spanish nose.

"I'm going for a short walk up the hill. Would you like to come, or may I take Maria Sophia to see the donkeys." She caught the glance between Esti and Sergio.

"Of course. Please return within one hour."

"I will." She knelt down beside Maria Sophia's chair. "Would you like to come visit the donkeys with me?"

The little girl bounced down from her chair, took her stuffed donkey from the table and took Anne's hand.

"Let's go, then." And they walked away. Her back tensed, waiting for a shot or a blow or a hand pulling her back into the plaza. Cold ran up her spine. When they turned the corner and trudged up the long hill towards the pasture, she relaxed.

"Is it a very long way?"

"Not too long. Would it be okay if I called you by your secret name?"

"Yes."

"Okay, Naomi. We'll be at the donkeys soon."

* * *

When Anne and Maria Sophia had walked off, Esti said, "Colette called."

"So?"

"They are considering the problem of the commander."

"What does that mean?" He reached over and tucked an errant lock of hair behind her ear.

"They don't want to leave any loose ends here. The woman, too. She took a photo of Maria Sophia the other day. At least take her phone."

"No woman, no phone." Sergio called the waiter over and ordered a spritz. Esti shook her head when the waiter asked her.

"No mess, they insist."

"What about the guy she sits with?" Sergio said.

"He was here long before she came. Don't worry about him."

"The plan was stupid, to hide the child in plain view of everyone."

Stupid. Perhaps it would have been easier to hold her in a remote farmhouse somewhere, and to take her closer to the time of the vote they wanted to go their way. But no, the bosses wanted her here, in plain sight.

"It has gone on too long."

"Why did you take her so early?" he asked.

"The bosses wanted other concessions from the child's grandfather. The vote is the final thing."

"Did he do what they asked?"

"Yes, but he wants the daily proof of life in return."

"What sort of accident shall we arrange for the commander?"

"I think he should kill himself while cleaning his gun," Esti said.

"No, a car I think. He goes out to the country every afternoon to ride a horse for an hour. The road runs along the river. It will be easy to force him over the side." Sergio leaned back in his chair when the waiter approached with his drink. He raised glass in Esti's direction and she blew him a kiss.

"What if he doesn't die?" she said.

"He will die. When I run down to check on him and call for the ambulance, I'll make sure."

"I don't—"

"I've done this in the past."

"When?"

"This afternoon."

"Very well." She stretched across the table and kissed him.

"Don't fail," she whispered into his ear. "They don't like failure."

* * *

When they reached the pasture with the three donkeys and the foal, Anne took some sugar cubes from a bag in her purse and clucked to them.

"If you put your hand out with sugar in it, they'll take it from you," she said.

"I'm scared they will bite me."

"They're very nice. I'll show you."

The curious soft gaze of one of the Jennies met hers. She patted the animal's nose and held out her hand for the gentle rasp of her tongue.

"May I try."

Polite, Anne thought. Good manners at four years old.

"Yes. Are you four years old, Naomi?"

"Five." She put her hand out to the colt. He nuzzled her hand and took the sugar cube. Naomi giggled.

"It feels funny."

They fed all their sugar cubes; the donkeys returned to grazing. Anne checked her watch. Just two minutes left. A car passed, the only one in the last quarter hour. Where was he? Could they have suspected him? Was he sitting in that Guardia office, the commander with the lofty nose threatening him. "We have to go," Anne said. It was time. Fifteen minutes, he said. It was twenty minutes now.

"Just another minute. Please."

"Just another minute."

A black Mercedes drove by and parked. Daniel got out and walked over to them.

"It's my friend, Daniel," Anne said. He knelt down to talk to Naomi in what Anne knew must be Hebrew. Naomi's soft hand crept into hers.

"I've told her we're going to take her home to Israel, to her mommy and daddy." Naomi looked a question up at Anne.

"Naomi, I think we should go with Daniel. It's time to take you away from Esti. Will you come with us?"

"I will."

They walked back to the Mercedes, Anne buckled Naomi into the car seat in the back and they drove off.

"In twenty minutes." Anne heard the fear in her own voice. She coughed and tried again.

"In twenty minutes they'll expect me back."

"They'll start looking in thirty." Thirty minutes and then what or who?

"The police?"

"An hour after that, but not for kidnapping. It'll be something else, but they will be looking for you and the child alone. Not with me."

The hills, some of them planted in olive trees, rose on either side of the car, high above the brown river. A warrant for her. The hills swirled green and grey past her window. She gripped her hands into fists and lowered her head to meet them.

"Anne?"

"A little dizzy."

"We have to follow the plan and all will be well."

The warrant wouldn't be for him. Why did she agree to this?

"How long to drive to Barcelona?"

"Ten hours."

"We'll have to stop. She can't stand ten hours."

"We'll stop in Manzanares but we have to go through the mountains first."

Mountains. Her favorite.

CHAPTER 10

Esti checked her watch. Where were they? Esti returned to her table and called the waiter over.

"Juanito, who has donkeys?"

"Donkeys?"

"Yes, donkeys. That woman took Naomi to see donkeys. Where are they?"

"A pasture up on the mountain has donkeys."

"What road?"

"Calle Cerillo."

Esti raced out of the plaza, up the steep road to the pasture. By the time she reached the field, the donkeys were alone.

* * *

Sergio stood on the side of a lane that overlooked the riding stables and gave him quick access to the road the commander would take. He leaned against the car and let the sun play over his face. He'd be glad to get out of this province and back to Madrid where he belonged, away from this do-nothing town and Esti with her commands. It was getting harder to pretend to be in love with her, to touch her and kiss her, to convince people all was normal. She repulsed him, with her *Basque* accent and her need to control the operation. And now he had to kill a Guardia commander. That would be on him, his record. He heard his mother's voice telling him God tallied his deeds. Superstition, he thought. Rubbish. He shook his head and trained his binoculars on the road below.

The commander drove out through the gates of the stables and made the right turn towards Setenil. Soon he would pass the side-road where Sergio waited. In five kilometers the road curved above an arroyo where he would force him over the cliff to the river. He got into his truck and turned the key. The sweat from his palms slicked the steering wheel and he used the tail of his shirt to wipe it down. His right leg, poised to hit the gas pedal, trembled.

His phone buzzed. Her again. What was it now? He could ignore the call and tell her later he was out of range. He answered.

"What?"

"The child is missing. We may need him. Get back here to the plaza as soon as you can."

* * *

A few minutes after leaving the donkey pasture, Daniel drove through hills cultivated with smokey-green olive trees. Far above, a yellow tractor, its driver dark and featureless, mowed the grass between the trees.

"How will they search for us?" she asked.

"It depends on whether or not the information about the safe houses has been compromised. They believe there's a mole in our organization."

Anne gasped as though his words punched air from her lungs but caught herself before she screamed her questions at him.

"A mole! How long? How long have you known this? That changes everything, Daniel." Not a scream, but a note of hysteria crept into her voice. "What will we do?"

"Carry on while they ferret out the mole. Our next stop is Manzanares. I'll call again."

A red convertible passed them, top down in spite of the chill in the air. Anne caught a glimpse of the driver's face. Thomas? Was that Thomas? She swung round but the car had disappeared around a curve.

"Did you see the driver of that car?"

"The Fiat? No."

"He looked like Thomas."

"Do you expect him?" He glanced at her and then back at the road.

"No, no. Daniel, did he arrange for you to find me?" Did Thomas throw her into this? Why was he here, driving into Setenil?

"No. Why do you ask?" His head swung towards her.

"How did you find me?"

"Would you believe a coincidence?"

"No."

"I thought you showed promise and when we needed someone expert with children who might be sympathetic, I thought of going to Canada to ask you. When we investigated, we found you planned a trip to Spain all ready. We...encouraged your travel agent to suggest Setenil."

"The last time I use her." She thought Trudy was a friend.

"Yes. It only took a small sum. What did you think had happened?"

"I thought maybe Thomas—"

"No. He's a good man but we didn't need him. I was told you and he were no longer a couple. You flew back from Bermuda with him. What happened since then?"

Anne kept her face to the side-window, watching hills the color of rosemary climb beside the road. "He didn't tell me about his shadow life."

"How could he?"

"How could he not?"

"He smuggled women and children out of Afghanistan when their lives were threatened and found them safe haven in the USA. Secrecy was paramount."

"Why didn't he tell me?" Her eyes sought his but he kept them focussed on the road.

"Because we don't tell anyone anything about the mission."

"Anne." The tiny voice called her from the back seat.

"Yes, Sweetpea."

"Are you and Daniel fighting?"

"No, we aren't. Are you scared?"

"No. But I'm thirsty."

"In the bag," Daniel said.

Anne passed a yellow sport bottle to Naomi.

"Tell me when you're finished."

She replaced the bag at her feet.

"How long to Manzanares?"

"Four hours."

"We'll need to stop before then." Little bladders and little legs meant stops. "Are you taking an AutoRoute?"

"No. Longer, but unexpected by anyone trying to find us."

"More places to stop on the AutoRoute."

71

"Why do you want to stop?" He sounded irritated. No children in his life, she thought.

"The child—"

"We can't."

"We must. She has to move about, go to the bathroom, and eat. Surely you or the people who planned this considered the needs of a small child?" Naomi bumped her shoulder with the juice bottle and Anne replaced it in the bag.

"Perhaps not enough. Give me a little warning."

"Every hour should do it."

"Every hour?"

"Yes. This is why you brought me, Daniel. In one hour, stop somewhere that I can take her to the bathroom. What haven't you told me about this mission?"

"Nothing."

She gripped her hands until her knuckles hurt. Nothing, except now the string of houses weren't safe and they had no one to back them up if the mission itself were compromised.

CHAPTER 11

When Esti returned to the plaza, Sergio sat at their usual table, eating tapas of anchovies on toast. She detested anchovies.

"You didn't find them?" he said. He'd ordered her a glass of red wine, the local *tinto*, even though she preferred white. She called the waiter to take it away.

"No, I didn't find them. She's taken the child and now I have to call that woman in Switzerland."

"Should I look around a little first?"

"No." She tapped her long red fingernails on her phone, and then pushed the speed-dial for the office in Switzerland.

Moments later Colette picked up the call. "Yes? What is it, Esti." she said.

Esti gripped the phone, fighting the urge to pitch it across the cafe. The last job for her and her bosses. No more taking instructions given by a judgemental bitch sitting with a headset in a safe office in Geneva. Esti shook the phone and answered.

"The child is missing. She went for a walk with a woman from the plaza and hasn't returned."

"How long?"

"Thirty minutes."

Silence. Say something, anything.

"Are you still there?"

"I am awaiting instructions."

More silence.

"Esti, the Guardia commander must issue a bulletin for her, fraud or identity-theft. Nothing that would cause them to think she was dangerous and nothing about the child being taken. Say she has been seen with a child, not your child."

"What if he won't?"

"He took a bribe. He will. Await instructions. We will tell you a likely destination in a short while."

"Yes."

"Where is Sergio?"

"He's here with me." Sergio shook his head, violently. Was he afraid she was giving the phone to him?

"He should speak to the commander. Make sure the commander knows Sergio followed him today. We want him afraid."

"Very well. What about the grandfather and his demands for daily proof of life?"

"Our employer's concern, but I expect he will be told we have lost patience with him and the child's welfare depends solely on the vote."

"He won't accept that." They must be crazy. Would the grandfather comply without proof the child was alive?

"Keep your phone on."

She rushed over to Winston's table but he denied knowing Anne's last name. Not likely, Esti thought. These people, these English, always introduce themselves. The woman wasn't English though. Maybe she didn't want to tell her last name.

Esti returned to her table, sat down and leaned forward to whisper to Sergio.

"She wants you to talk to the commander, but I shall see him first. Afterwards, this is what I want you to tell him."

A few minutes later, Sergio left the plaza. Esti hurried away in the opposite direction.

* * *

Thomas downshifted to take the hill and increased speed when he left the curve, passing a black Mercedes driving from Setenil. He missed the driver's face and the side windows were tinted.

He parked his red Fiat on the street near the bus stop and strolled up to the plaza. Overhead loomed the famous outcroppings of rock. A lone man sat at a table against the wall, watching him from the moment he entered the cafe. Police, he wondered, or cautious.

He ordered a glass of the local red wine and nodded to the other man.

"Good afternoon," said Winston.

"Afternoon. May I join you for a moment?"

"Of course."

Thomas shifted to a chair opposite Winston and reached across the table to shake his hand.

"I'm Thomas Beauchamp. I wonder if you can help me?"

"Winston Caldwell. Do you need help finding a place to stay in Setenil?"

"No, I'm here to visit a friend who's taken a house for a month or so. Perhaps you met her—Anne McPhail?"

"Yes, I have." Winston's eyes narrowed and he tilted his chair back against the stone wall.

"Have you any idea where she lives?"

A shutter came down over Winston's face. "She didn't tell you her address?"

"No. She doesn't know I'm coming. I think she may need a little help." Would Anne have confided in this man, or was he an agent or a kidnapper? He waited. The smell of frying *chorizo* and potato drifted across form the cafe. When the waiter bustled up with his drink, he ordered tapas of the fresh tortilla.

"You think she's in trouble?" Winston said.

"Or not yet in trouble."

A couple across the cafe from them caught Thomas's eye. They seemed to be having a violent argument in whispers. The dark-haired young woman slammed her hand on the table, took out her phone and dialled. Moments later she rushed over to Winston's table.

"Senor Caldwell, that woman, that Anne, she took Maria Sophia for a walk and she hasn't come back. It's been more than an hour, almost an hour and a half. I think she abducted her."

"I don't think she's the type to abduct a child, Esti. She's a children's doctor."

Esti twisted her mouth and tossed her long hair. She wasn't buying that one, Thomas thought.

"So she says. I'm going to call the Guardia. What is her last name?"

"I have no idea. We are not on those terms."

"You must. You talk to her every day. Tell me her last name." She pounded the table and leaned towards Winston, her dark eyes daring him to lie to her. Air snorted from her nostrils and her voice quivered with anger.

"Esti, if I knew her last name, I would tell you."

"I shall call the Guardia." She ran back to her table and resumed her angry whisper to Sergio. Moments later, he left her and strode out of the plaza.

* * *

Esti marched into the Guardia office, and slammed the door behind her. Heads came up from behind the reception desk, two men stood up from desks in the main area of the room, hands on their sidearms. She tossed her hair and spoke to the officer behind the desk.

"I must speak to the commander immediately."

"Why?"

She felt a surge of anger and heat rushed to her face. "Tell him Esti is here."

"He'll want to know why."

"He will know."

A smirk drifted across the officer's face. He buzzed the office and spoke, and waved her through to the office. Stupid clod. She closed the door and stood against it, struggling to get control of herself before she spoke. The commander raised his head.

"Why are you here?"

"The child is gone. Taken."

"What? Who?"

"I think a new tourist. An Englishwoman."

"I'll see."

He checked the passports registered as British. "No Englishwoman recently."

"Come to the plaza. That Cantrell. She sits at his table every day."

"But—"

"Come."

77

He followed her out the door, past his staff and their leers. A few minutes later they marched into the plaza to Winston's table.

"Senor Caldwell."

"Yes, Commander." Winston tilted his chair back and squinted against the sun.

"We are looking for the woman who takes coffee with you every morning."

"Yes?"

"Where is she?" Esti slammed her fists on the table. A glass tipped over and spilled water over the side, dripping on her shoes. She pushed it aside and it crashed onto the stones, splintering.

"I have no idea."

The commander jerked his head towards Esti. "This one says you won't tell the woman's last name."

"True. She didn't tell me."

"The English always introduce themselves," Esti said, tossing her hair and hitting the table again.

"Do control yourself, Esti. Juanito has enough work to do. She's not English."

"Not English." The commander turned to Esti. "You said she was English."

"They all sound the same to me."

"I will search through the passports again. I thought we were looking for an Englishwoman." He paced away but turned back.

"Was she the woman you brought to the office?"

"Yes."

"A Canadian. Come, Esti. We will look at the passports." He grabbed her arm but she shrugged him off and stomped away beside him.

CHAPTER 12

When Esti and the commander left, Thomas said, "You don't know her last name?" He raised one eyebrow.

"Not a syllable."

"Perhaps we should talk somewhere else?"

"Would you care to see my villa?"

"I would."

Winston's villa sat on the cliff-side of a street clinging to the hill above the plaza. The overhang of rock seemed to consume the houses across the street but light and air surrounded his whitewashed villa under a red-tiled roof. A weather-beaten green door opened into a sun-filled living room.

"Not a cave-dweller, then?" Thomas said.

They sat at a marble-topped table on the terrace overlooking the river. Winston turned his face up to the sun.

"I didn't leave England to live in the dark in Spain."

"Why Setenil then?"

"A question for another day. Anne?"

"Yes. Who's she's been talking to?"

Winston opened his eyes and said, "Besides me?"

"Yes."

"A new man appeared one day in the cafe but I never saw his face. I think he dropped by her place at least once and chatted with her about the child, but she never said his name."

"Did she seem to trust him?"

"I wasn't sure. She was a bit bothered."

A bit bothered. Thomas stood at the terrace wall. He turned his back on the town.

"What did she want to do?"

"She wanted to talk to the Guardia but whoever it was told her the commander was corrupt. I advised her the laws against slander here are strict and to be cautious what she said about people. Might I offer you a glass of wine?"

"No... Yes, thanks. So she didn't want to involve the police?"

Winston left the table, walked back into the house and returned a few moments later with two glasses and a bottle of red wine.

"She thinks she saw the commander take a bribe from Esti's boyfriend," he said. He popped the cork from the bottle, poured a small amount, swirled it, and then tasted . He passed a glassful to Thomas.

"A bribe to do what?"

"Whatever protection they needed, I suppose. Who are you?"

"That question comes a little late, doesn't it? I'm Anne's friend. What work do you do?"

"I'm a retired photojournalist. Travel mostly. I still dabble at times. And you?"

A cover, Thomas thought, but for what?

"I'm a businessman from Vermont. I may need help looking for her."

"You're going to follow her?"

"Yes. If she calls me..." Thomas tapped his fingers on the table.

"I may be able to help."

"Do you know where she lives?"

"Yes. Take the street to the north out of the terrace cafe and you'll come to a villa with a blue door. The owner is a British woman called Metcalf."

"Thanks." Thomas stood up, shook Winston's hand and hurried down to the house with the blue door.

A few minutes later, Thomas was inside. Dark, he thought. Strange place for Anne to pick to live. She loved the light. He switched on a table lamp and checked the kitchen. A full stock of food. She hadn't expected to go anywhere. Upstairs, he found her suitcases neatly stacked in a corner and her nightgown tucked under a pillow. He held it to his face, breathing in her scent for a moment.

He searched for her wallet and her passport but both were gone. The house was left as though she would return any moment but she took her identification. He didn't find her return ticket either although he knew she had one. Tradecraft, he thought. Ari's plan and she's gone with him. But where?

If the stranger were Ari, he'd have a safe house or a string of them, waiting for their arrival. Would Quin find out for him? Did Winston have the resources to get the information? He'd try both.

* * *

Sergio loitered across from the Guardia office until he saw the commander leave for his afternoon visit to the cafe. He caught up to him in a few strides.

"Commander."

"Why are you talking to me here in the street? What are you thinking?" The commander swung around to confront him.

"I'm thinking you're lucky to be alive. The road you take to the horse barns is very dangerous. Walk with me." He fell in beside the policeman.

"What... Are you trying to intimidate me?" He stopped and stepped closer to Sergio who was shorter and lighter.

"I don't have to. I all ready bought you and it's time for you to act."

"Not here in the street. Come back to my office."

"Fuck that. We'll go up to the vineyards. No talking until we get away from the town."

They took the next turn. Steps climbed between two rock overhangs to the street above. The fence across the road enclosed the pasture with the donkeys.

"What do you want?"

"We need you to put out a bulletin for that woman Anne, who lives in Mrs. Metcalf's house."

"What charge?"

"Think of something. Fraud or identity theft. Something serious but nonviolent. We want you to find her, not kill her."

"Why?"

"You don't need to know why, just do the paperwork." Sergio moved closer to the commander who stepped back, stumbling over a rock.

"And if I won't."

"I recorded our deals and remember the dangerous road." The commander's face drained of color. How did this coward get to be a commander in the Guardia?

"I'll do it when I get back, but I'll want more money."

"No more money, but I may let you keep your job."

The commander took a few steps away.

"Are you coming back with me?" he said.

"No."

Sergio waited until the commander had disappeared back down the steps before he texted Esti to tell her it was done.

* * *

Anne rested her head against the seat and closed her eyes. She thought she slept until a little voice piped into her ear. She looked at Naomi who napped beside her.

"I have to pee-pee."

"Daniel, we have to stop soon. Naomi has to go to the bathroom."

"There's a town coming up."

Ahead Anne could see a cathedral high on a hill, its minaret-shaped turrets shining pink in the late-day sun. A whitewashed town huddled below the church. Daniel pulled off the road to a filling station and Anne hustled Naomi into the facilities. On the way back she bought sandwiches, coffee and milk, convincing the girl behind the counter that she only wanted cheese, no ham. She bought a guidebook in English from a rack near the cash.

The road north ran beside the Lantuela Natural Reserve, a wetland that had been extensive in the past but agricultural practices had reduced it to only nine hundred hectares from what had been hundreds of square kilometers. Efforts were underway to restore the habitat and prevent the two saltwater lakes from drying up. In the rushes at the roadside she saw the familiar emerald heads of mallard ducks.

They stopped several more times on the road north and then east, travelling through hills, approaching Manzanares towards nine in the evening. Naked granite hills, lit by an orange sunset loomed over the town. A pink-stone fortress appeared out of the darkness of the town. In the distance, Anne could hear music as the lighting changed on the castle turrets. *Son et Lumiere*, she thought. The story of the town played out in lights and music at the castle.

"Where will we stay tonight?" Anne asked.

"I thought we might drive straight through." Daniel glanced at her.

"No. She's been very good but she is tired and hungry and needs a bath and sleep."

"We'll have to ask her to say we're her grandparents."

"She can do that."

Anne woke Naomi who dozed again in the car seat beside her.

"Naomi, we have to stop and go into a place where we can sleep tonight. I think you should use special names for Daniel and me. Can you call me Nanna and Daniel, Poppa? Just for a little while?"

"Why?"

"It's a game so no one can find us. But it's a secret game." She's only five, Anne thought. How long could she keep from calling her Anne?

"Okay."

But Naomi didn't have to call them anything. She fell asleep on Daniel's shoulder while he carried her across the pavement of the parking lot, avoiding holes and chunks of concrete heaved up by recent road work. Anne carried their backpacks and Naomi's donkey.

The dark-haired man behind the reception desk handed them a key with his left hand. The right one lay on the desk where he had placed it, pale and inert. Paralysis, Anne thought. A pair of aluminum crutches stood against a wall behind him.

"Breakfast is 7 a.m. to 10 a.m.," he said, pointing to a sign on the desk.

One look at the rusted door of the elevator and Daniel took the stairs.

The door opened into a Spartan two-bedded room enlivened by bright scarlet coverlets, but lit by the usual forty-watt bulbs of Spanish hotels. The bathroom held a shower and a tub clean enough that she could bathe Naomi.

Daniel went down and talked the dining room staff into letting him bring dinner up for Naomi and Anne, and two hours later they slept. Daniel made a call just before she went to sleep, but to whom and for what she didn't know.

* * *

Later in the afternoon, Thomas walked through tunnel of rock to the cafe. Winston sat with his back to the wall, his craggy face flushed red by the setting sun.

"Did you find what you needed?" Winston asked.

"She's gone; planned to go, I think. Her passport, her tickets and money are missing but her clothes are still there. If she's on the run with Ari, they'll need a safe house or several to wait for the agents to come for them."

"So in the wind."

"Maybe not, if I can get a list of the safe houses."

"Do you have the contacts to do that?" Winston leaned across the table.

"Do you?"

The waiter arrived at the table before Winston answered, took the order and hurried away. Winston sat back against the wall and closed his eyes.

"Do you?" Thomas repeated his question.

"How could I?"

"You've poked around the world, met some people."

"Who are you?"

"A worried man."

Winston opened his eyes, made brief contact with Thomas's, and moved them away to search the patio once again. "Don't count on me. Work your own contacts but I'll make a call."

Two Guardia officers walked into the plaza. Winston's gaze followed them into the cafe and he looked at Thomas.

"I'd get out of here, if I were you."

"And you?"

"I'm an old hand here. Go."

Thomas hurried out of the plaza, reached his car and took the highway towards Ronda. He stopped at Acinipo, a Roman ruin five kilometers from Ronda, parked in the empty lot and made a call to Quin. While he waited, he hiked up the hillside, past a partially-restored amphitheater to where the cliff fell away in a precipitous drop to the floor of the valley perhaps five hundred meters below. A bright yellow tractor, a toy in the vast landscape, worked a field. In the distance the rocky hills gave way to the Sierra. White villages dotted along the mountains shone in the last rays of the sun. Thomas hurried down before the east wind brought rain, darkness overtook him and turned a pleasant track into a treacherous path.

His phone played "Sunday Morning".

"Quin?"

"Tom. What do you need?"

"A list of Mossad safe houses in this part of Spain and the south of France."

"I'm supposed to get those how?"

Thomas pushed mute and swore.

"Come on, Quin. Work a contact or two."

"Ari was my contact."

"Ask someone else. Anne needs help." Where else could he turn? After long seconds, Quin answered.

"I'll see what I can do. Where will you be?"

"Barcelona."

"Why?"

"He can't go through North Africa and they'll be watching the airports for Anne."

"I'll call you back."

Thomas drove the few kilometers to Ronda. Darkness fell, but he went on, for the ten hours it took to reach Barcelona, and Anne.

* * *

A few minutes after leaving Winston, Esti and the commander peered at the computer screen in his office.

"Is this the woman?"

"I think so. The picture isn't good. What's her name?"

"Anne McPhail. She's the only Canadian woman registered here on her own. She is living in Ms. Metcalf's house."

"We must find her. Sergio told you what to do. Put out an alert for her for extortion and fraud, but say 'don't apprehend but keep under observation because you're trying to find her bosses.' Tell me all the sightings."

"How will you decide which are genuine?"

"Write it up." She waited by the window in his office, curling her nose against the smell of his expensive French cologne. When he finished, she took the bulletin from his hand and read it.

"That will do."

"I should get some more money," he said. "After all, I didn't know you were going to kidnap a child and hold her here all this time." He moved closer to her, and flicked a strand of her hair with one finger.

"You have received enough money."

"I would take something else." Esti twisted away, hiding her disgust at the thought of him touching her.

"Perhaps...after the woman has been found."

"If she dies—"

"You would be quiet. The people I work for are very powerful."

"I have some power also."

"Do you have a place in the country, for later, after we find her." His pupils dilated and she heard his breathing quicken. Later, she thought, his eyes would widen and mouth hang open when she fired into his ironed shirt. He would clutch at the wound to hold back the blood.

He pawed at her but she slipped out of his grasp and stood with her hand on the door.

"Send the bulletin and I'll give you my private number."

They walked together to the desk. He told the clerk to distribute the bulletin.

"I'll wait for your call," she said, handing him her card.

* * *

Later, she spoke to Colette. "The woman's name is Anne McPhail."

"Are you certain?"

"Yes. Who is she?"

"She's interfered with us before, in Bermuda. It would be best if she didn't get a third opportunity."

"I'll make sure."

"See that you do."

CHAPTER 13

Day Ten

Daniel's voice, hissing in Anne's ear, woke her from a dreamless sleep.

"What?"

"We have to leave before the staff comes in. There's an alert for you: identity theft. I have to get you to Barcelona for a new passport."

"That was fast."

"The commander."

"As I said." She shook off her anger and woke Naomi up, washed her face and brushed her teeth and told her they were going but it was still night.

"Is Daniel coming?"

"Of course."

A few minutes later, she crept down the stairs with Naomi on her hip, one tiny arm thrown across her shoulders. Daniel needed his hands free, he said. Free for what, she thought.

The empty lobby reassured her but Daniel hustled her out the door. She followed him across the parking lot, checking ahead of her before she took each step, remembering the potholes and the chunks of concrete littering her path. She hit her shin on a protruding copper pipe but swallowed her yelp of pain.

She settled Naomi in the car seat and sat beside her.

"You're sitting in the back?" Daniel said.

"For now. How long?"

"Six or seven hours if we don't stop much."

"Six or seven times, unless she sleeps."

"Should we get something to give her?"

"No."

"But—"

"No."

An hour later, after driving through the *Sierra Calderones*, a low mountain range, they took the ramp from the *Autovia del Mediterraneo*—the A-7—to Sagunto, another town shining white in the early-morning sun. They stopped at a service station, gassed up, had a quick breakfast of pastry and coffee and re-joined the AP-7, the toll road to Barcelona. Once a patrol car followed long enough to check their license plate.

"Whose car is this?" Anne asked.

"A rental from the UK that entered a week ago with a man, woman and child onboard. Don't worry, Anne. Everything is in order."

"Except my passport."

"We'll look after that in Barcelona."

Anne sank back in her seat beside Naomi. What had she done? Perhaps she could call Thomas at the next stop and ask him to come to Spain. But would he? She hadn't encouraged him to think they had a future the last time they spoke.

"I'd like to call Thomas," she said.

"Wait until Barcelona. We'll have new names, new documents and new phones."

So simple for him. He likely changed identities many times a year but she had only one. Naomi's hand slipped into hers. It must be the right thing to do. It must.

* * *

That afternoon, in Setenil, Winston sat on the terrace of his villa, his feet on the table beside a glass of red wine. His phone rang, the call he expected from Lyon.

"Good afternoon, Henri."

"It is so good to hear from you, old friend. What can I do for you?"

"Perhaps to meet?" He sipped, waiting for the answer.

"Where?"

"Barcelona. I can be there in four hours."

"Where would you like to meet?"

"The airport would do, at the Portaguia Restaurant? We could have dinner."

"I'll be there."

Winston poured the last of his wine into the potted rosemary that sat by his chair and hurried out to his car. He asked his online assistant to book him on the flight to Barcelona from Malaga and settled back for the drive through the mountains to the coast.

Halfway, he pulled over to a lookout. Five white villages nestled against the dark forests and rocky outcrops of the mountains, ablaze in the setting sun. He never failed to stop and appreciate the view, unique in Spain. After a few moments he resumed his drive.

At 7 p.m. he gave Henri's name to the *maitre d'* and followed him to a table for two in a windowed alcove. Henri sat with his back to the panoramic view of the airport. He waved a careful hand. A sleek fifty-year-old, his still-dark hair brushed away from a high forehead, he wore a dinner jacket constructed to hide a mild paunch and narrow shoulders and a holster. Winston knew he had been one of the most dangerous operatives in Europe before he retired to his desk job.

Henri's approach to dining bordered on religious rite, so no business until the evening was closing with snifters of cognac.

"And so, why have we enjoyed this magnificent dinner?"

"I need a fact."

"Just one? Four hours and all this for one fact." He waved a hand to take in the table and the restaurant and raised a quizzical eyebrow.

"One."

"Ask, and we shall see."

Winston waited a moment. Did he want to be indebted to Interpol to help a woman he barely knew?

* * *

By 3 a.m. Thomas arrived in Barcelona. He remembered a hotel called Hotel Sagrada Familia close to the cathedral. Only a few rooms, no more than eighty or so and some with a terrace, the hotel was popular with businessmen and others like himself with more ambiguous purposes. He collapsed on the bed, under the cheerful red cover and slept.

Late in the afternoon, waiting for a call from Winston or Quin, he strolled for the three minutes it took to get to the cathedral park. He slipped inside the cathedral and sat in a pew, taking in the fabulous and fantastic architecture and decoration.

Later, he stood before tiers of votive candles, their light shining scarlet through the holders. He took a taper, lit a candle and prayed for Anne's safety. The first time he'd prayed in years. Above him soared columns reaching to the stained glass windows, dwarfed by the immense space. Behind him a mass was beginning. He sat in a back pew and lost himself in the familiar sounds. When the moment came for communion, he left, strolling past the line of tourists snaking into Sagrada Familia.

He darted across the avenue into a park with a view of the facade with its turrets, each with its cone of colorful ceramic fruit, and sat on a bench beside the gravel path. The time to build a cathedral was measured, not in years, but in generations of patient believers who came to mass in the midst of construction for all their lives. The peace of the church drifted away and he tapped on his phone, willing Quin or Winston to call him, to tell him where she had gone. A grey sparrow settled into the dust near his feet, pecking at a few crumbs dropped by a passing child. He moved his foot slowly towards it, rewarded when it hopped on his shoe and gazed up at him.

"Nothing here for you, little bird."

But the phone didn't ring, and he waited through the long night and the long day that followed.

* * *

In mid-afternoon, Daniel navigated to the beachfront in Barcelona.

Barcelona, the capital of Catalonia was the second largest city in Spain. Buildings by Modernist architects like Gaudi and Domenech i Montaner drew hundreds of thousands of tourists to the city every year. Because it was the largest city on the Mediterranean, cruise ships clogged its harbor and their passengers its streets year-round.

They abandoned the car on a street near the harbor and walked to the beach. Warm onshore breezes from the Balearic Sea ruffled Naomi's auburn hair. She'd been sleeping on Daniel's shoulder, but wiggled to get down and run along the sand. Anne took off her shoes and walked hand-in-hand with Daniel behind Naomi as she ran close to the wavelets and back again, laughing happily each time a wave touched her toes.

They stopped at a shore-side cafe, tempted by the aroma of fish, strung along sticks, roasting upright in front of an open fire and ate mounds of calamari and French fries and salad.

"Are you okay here on the beach alone for a half an hour or so?" he said.

"I don't have any money. I assume I shouldn't use an ATM."

"Yes. Don't." He passed her a neat stack of twenty euro notes he took from a money-belt and she stuffed them in her purse.

"I'm going to need some clothes soon."

"When I get back."

"What about a car?"

"I'll bring one." He left and a chill, resistant to the sunshine and warm breezes ran through her.

Naomi and Anne played on the sand, digging holes and building sandcastles with a shovel and pail Anne bought from a beach-side vendor.

"Anne?"

"Yes, Sweetpea?"

"When are we going to Israel?" They hadn't told her they were going to Israel. She remembered.

"Soon, after we go to France."

"France?"

"It's a country on our way."

That satisfied her for the present, but if she were remembering, they'd have to coach her on what to say or at least what to call them. Anne and Daniel wouldn't do.

Daniel came back and ushered them into a plush Mercedes and drove to an apartment with a view of the Sagrada Familia, Antoni Gaudi's fabulous unfinished cathedral. Building it consumed forty years of his life. A park, dwarfed by the immense church, spread out across the road.

"They're still at work on the cathedral," Anne said.

"It's good someone's working," Daniel said. "Spain has the highest unemployment in the EU at the moment, especially among the youth."

"How much?"

"Fifty-six per cent."

"What an awful situation. So most of them would still be at home. I wonder about the World Bank and the IMF. Recovery on the backs of starving people and the young leads to disaster. Germany in 1933, for example."

"Twenty percent of Spaniards live below the poverty line."

"Has there been violence?" Anne asked. A group of young men in the park below played an impromptu game of soccer.

"Some. The organization that took Naomi stirs them up and weapons flow to them, too."

Anne turned her back on the window and the Cathedral.

"Did you get the passport?"

"Yes. I gave you Thomas's last name and your own middle name so you are Elizabeth Beauchamp, a Canadian from Toronto. Naomi is your granddaughter. Her name is her own, Naomi Shapiro, a common name in Israel. Will she call you *Safta?*"

Grandmother. "Yes, or *Safta* Elizabeth."

The passport looked genuine to her and Naomi had her own, and a letter of permission from her parents for Anne to take her to Europe, visiting Spain, France and Italy before arriving back in Israel. Daniel told her not to talk in the elevators in Barcelona and she waited until he unlocked the door of the hotel room and she settled Naomi in front of a television.

"The pictures?" she said, looking at the woman who might be her.

"Other people who look enough like you to pass."

"Why the other countries?"

"In case."

"I'm going to call Thomas."

"He may be compromised."

"His cell, you mean?"

"Yes."

So she couldn't call him, even to say good-bye. She locked the door to the bathroom behind her, turned on the shower and stood under it and sobbed.

After, she reached for the soap and ran it down her leg. A vivid bruise surrounded the scrape on her shin from the encounter with a copper pipe in the parking lot at Manzanares. The area around the wound was tender and swollen, more that she expected from the bruise. Infection? She hoped not.

* * *

Winston raised his cognac glass to the chandelier and swirled the amber liquid inside its fat belly.

"I met a woman, a Canadian, in Setenil. We sat together and drank wine and ate lunch and watched the other patrons of the cafe. She and I grew concerned about a child, a child with a nanny, whose parents were apparently out of the country. A strange little girl, called Maria Sophia, who played alone and sang in Hebrew to her dolls when her minder didn't stop her." He paused to sip.

"My new friend grew worried about her, but I suggested she overreacted. Then a man she trusted contacted her, a man to whom she owed a serious favor, who suggested the child was kidnapped. She did enough research on her own to convince herself and now my friend and Maria Sophia have disappeared."

"The fact?" Henri held up a finger to the waiter, asking for another cognac.

"The commander of the local Guardia issued a warrant for her arrest on fraud charges. The missing child is being ignored in the bulletin. I think my friend was correct. Now she has taken the child and is trying to return her to her parents."

"Did the parents pay the ransom?"

"I believe the kidnapping was for political reasons."

"Which you do not want to share with me."

"Better not, although you are as aware as I am of the tensions in the part of the world that speaks Hebrew."

"The one little fact?"

"Is the Guardia commander corrupt? Anne, my friend, thinks he took a bribe from the people holding the child. If Interpol leaned on him, I think he would give up the other two."

"This is a dossier you require, not one little fact. Who are the others?"

"A woman and a man. The woman is beautiful, *Basque* perhaps. The name she uses is Esti." Winston passed his phone with its clear picture of Esti and Sergio to Henri.

"A beautiful *Basque* woman, employed by whom? Who is the man?"

"I have an idea about whom she works for. The man appears to be her lover, but he bribed the commander."

Henri passed the phone back to Winston. "Send me the picture. Anne did this on her own?"

"Perhaps not entirely."

"Her accomplice?"

"Say her guardian. I don't know who he is, but an old friend of hers arrived who may work for that American agency." Winston took the last sip of his glass.

"Indeed. So many people chasing each other across Europe."

"And at the center a vulnerable child."

"What else is there for you?" Henri's eyes, hooded, searched his face.

"The cartel that employs Esti."

"Yes."

"It was responsible for my wife's death. I chased them all over Europe but I gave up, settled in Spain, and retired to contemplating world events from a disconnected place. But now, the cartel threatens someone else's family and a woman I care about. I want to bring it down."

"We have been trying since you retired."

"Without success."

"The woman in Switzerland is making mistakes. She hired the wrong person in Bermuda and now perhaps here. We will find her and bring the organization down."

Winston raised his glass in a silent toast to Interpol's success.

* * *

"We should take her out for a walk," Anne said. She brushed Naomi's wild curls into order and tied them with navy bows into ponytails on either side of her head.

"The Magic Fountains are fun for kids."

"The Magic Fountains?"

"A water course and a sound and light show. It was built for an exhibition or world fair or something at *Placa d' Espanya*."

"Can we eat there?"

"Yes. We'll take the metro."

An hour later, they exited the metro at *Placa d'Espanya*. Daniel picked up Naomi and settled her on his shoulders.

"It's much wider than I expected," Anne said. "More cars, too." Six lanes of traffic circled the fountain, their lights becoming a blur of cool white and scarlet.

"We're going around to number 6, to La Creme."

"A restaurant?"

"Pastries, buns, coffee. We can stop after the show at one of the restaurants near the hotel."

They sat in the window of the cafe, drinking espresso while Naomi picked her pastry into tiny sections, inspected each one and then ate those with pastry cream last.

"Do you have any children?" Anne asked.

100

"No. I have a friend in Haifa. Perhaps when I am finished with the organization I'll settle down with her."

"What work would you do?"

"My brother works our farm. I would like to join him, grow oranges and children."

Anne laughed. "In that order?"

"Yes. First the oranges so I can support the family."

"What is her name, the woman in Haifa?"

"Shoshana. What about you? Are you and Thomas a couple?" He gestured to the server, asking for two more espressos.

"We were, but now…"

"Why? Because he kept a secret?"

"It's part of his life."

"Shoshana thinks I work for an NGO. You were a doctor?"

"Yes. My husband died and I couldn't go on. Medicine took more energy than I had."

"And now? What do you do?"

"An aunt left me quite a bit of money, so I retired. Travel, genealogy. Amusing myself, I suppose. I haven't started to feel guilty yet. Although lately, with the murders, I haven't been all that amused, either."

"Murders? Plural?"

"Yes. The one in Bermuda and two others in Culvers Mills, Thomas's home town in Vermont."

Daniel studied her face so closely she wondered if he was trying to decide whether he had allied himself with a mad woman.

"Three murders. Who were killed?"

"The first was a librarian, a blackmailer killed by one of her victims, the second an art thief and then the boy in Bermuda."

"So nothing to do with you?"

"Yes."

He relaxed back into his chair but asked another question. "What will you do? You're too young to retire, I think."

"I don't know. First I have to survive this journey."

A tug at her arm reminded Anne that Naomi was listening.

"Yes, Naomi?"

"Juice, please."

Later, they walked around the plaza to the towers at the entrance to the gardens leading to the National Palace of Montjuic. Colored lights turned the fountains, pulsating to music, into a fairyland. Water cascaded down from the Palace in a moving tapestry of purple and gold. Naomi squealed and bounced on Daniel's shoulders.

At the end of the evening and a supper in the hotel restaurant, Anne tucked Naomi into bed and lay down beside her.

"Naomi, can you remember something important?"

"Yes."

"Can you call me 'Safta' and Daniel, 'Saba'?"

"Yes. But I have *Safta* and *Saba* all ready."

"I know, but we're extra. Can you remember?"

"Yes."

She was remembering more and more, Anne thought. At least now she was sure they had the right child and hadn't kidnapped some innocent mother's baby.

CHAPTER 14

Day Eleven

Sergio stood in the park opposite the *Placa de la Sagrada Familia*, swearing into his cellphone.

"That bitch lost them! How could she lose them? I thought she was tracking the woman's mobile."

"Dead. No trace of them in Barcelona, but we have a list of the *Mossad* safe houses. We think someone is helping her and they'll turn up at one of the houses. Rent a fast car and drive to Montpellier. I'm texting you the address."

"Montpellier. Are you sure?" The bells of the cathedral started to ring for noon. His mother would be on her way home from mass, to make a tortilla for lunch for his little brother, the last one at home.

"Nothing is sure."

"What about Barcelona?"

"They are ahead of you—"

"Whose fault is that?" He loped out of the park and across to the cathedral door, taking the entrance marked for members of the congregation. When he went home, he would tell Mamma he lit a candle for her in La Sagrada Familia. The votives rose in scarlet ranks before the Virgin.

"Go to Montpellier."

"What is the assignment?"

"Elimination."

"The child too?" He dropped two coins in the collection box and took a taper and held it to the flame of a candle. The light through the holder stained his hand red.

"Yes, the child too. Do it, Sergio."

"What a waste." He lit another candle, this one for himself, made the sign of the cross, and left, avoiding the Virgin's gaze, but he knew she watched him to the door.

In Setenil, Esti put down the phone and then dialled again.

"Colette, we have a problem with Sergio. I think I should follow."

"Not for now. Stay in Setenil and keep up the appearance of a shocked nanny."

"If you insist."

"They do."

* * *

Early the next morning, Anne heard Daniel on the phone in the bathroom. When he came out, he stood at the side of the bed, looming over her like a Nordic giant.

"We're leaving," he said. "There's an alert for you with the picture from your passport. Remember you went to the police station, so they know which tourist you are."

"It doesn't look like me."

"We'll get you out of this."

"What are we doing?"

"After breakfast we'll take the bus for Perpignan

across the border in France. We'll get new mobile phones and dump these."

"The bus? Why? What happened to the Mercedes?"

"I abandoned it. We can't leave here in a stolen car with an alert out for you and Naomi. Too much risk."

Too much risk. Her chest started to burn and the room seemed oddly tilted.

"Anne, breathe."

Yes. Breathe. She was on the run with a madman who thought taking the local bus was safer than a fast car.

"Won't they be checking the buses?"

"Your papers are in order."

After breakfast, they took the Metro to *Placa D' Espanya* and then walked for ten minutes to Santos bus station. They passed a window decorated with sand and shells and tiny mannequins in shorts and bathing suits. She stopped in front.

"I'm going to buy her some more clothes and a little backpack."

"Do you have enough money?"

"Yes."

* * *

An hour later, they boarded the bus for Perpignan. Anne and Naomi sat together with Daniel across the aisle. Naomi hugged her new electric-pink backpack and a new doll with red hair and brown eyes. Anne studied a Hebrew-English dictionary, learning names for mother, father, grandparents, aunts and uncles.

"What will you call your dolly," Anne asked.

"Aliza."

"That's a pretty name."

An agent entered the bus, checking passports and identity cards.

"Why is he checking passports? We aren't even at the border and I thought it was borderless within the EU."

Daniel was looking away from her, out the window at a Guardia patrol car and the two officers standing by it. The agent stepped on board and ordered everyone off. Daniel patted the air downward. Did he want her to stay in her seat? Then she realized. He wanted them off last. She waited, letting a woman in a headscarf with five children in tow exit ahead of her.

Outside, women were screaming at the Guardia, demanding to know why their journeys were interrupted. The smaller children cried; the older ones chased each other around the patrol cars. A harassed officer spoke to Naomi, snuggled in Anne's arms.

"What is this lady's name?" he said in Spanish.

"*Safta* Elizabeth."

"*Safta*?" He asked Anne.

"Grandmother." How odd her voice sounded. Could he tell she was frightened?

"What language?"

"Hebrew."

"Do you have papers for the child?"

"Yes." Anne handed over the forged passport, the letter of permission and Naomi's school record from her preschool in Israel. Clever, Anne thought.

"Where are you taking her?"

"To visit her aunt in France and then to Rome to meet her parents."

"What is your aunt's name, Naomi."

"Your *doda*, Naomi." Anne translated.

"Doda Eliyana".

"Have a good journey," the agent said, and moved on to the next woman with a child.

Anne dug into her own backpack for bottle of juice and offered some to Naomi.

"No, thank you, *Safta*," she said, as the agent passed.

She edged to the back of the crowd, where Daniel leaned against the bus, bored, waiting for the melee to clear.

"Go," he said, not looking at her but at the Guardia. "Around the back into the hotel lobby. Don't run."

She walked, noticing the pain in her leg when she carried Naomi for a moment. She set her down but held tight to her hand. Her back arched, expecting a blow or a restraining hand at any moment. Her heart raced, urging her to run. Where was she supposed to go? What was she doing here? How did she get involved with this mad plan?

Ahead of her loomed the Barcelo hotel above the facade of the train station. Daniel appeared at her elbow, guided her to a cafe inside, sat and ordered juice for Naomi and a glass white wine for her.

"Too early," she said.

"You're very pale. I think you need it." She gripped the stem of the glass with both hands, took a small sip, shuddered and drank a little more.

"What now?"

"Wait here. I'll be back."

She ordered more juice for Naomi and a coffee for herself. Her heart returned to normal and she was able to breathe without gasping past the lump of fear in her throat. Light, admitted by tall window overlooking the city, bounced off the white tables and china. She relaxed, her shoulders dropped and she smiled at Naomi who sat beside her, singing softly to her donkey.

When Daniel returned he paid the waiter and led them across the parking lot to a blue van, the kind families bought because of the storage for soccer gear and hockey bags and kids.

"Ours?"

"It is now. I disabled the onboard computer."

"So no tracking?"

"I hope not."

She settled back into her seat. Her heart started to race again and she forced her breathing to slow, willing herself to calm down. What was the matter with her? She'd been in tight situations before.

"How long to Perpignan?"

"Not long. A little over an hour and a half."

The route took them along the coast, past charming fishing villages that Anne would have liked to dawdle in for hours. But Daniel stayed on the toll road and took one of the only two exits to Perpignan.

In Perpignan, Daniel parked on a side street, left the keys in the van and then hurried them in front of the train station with its fallen man statue of Dali on the roof. He stopped beside a black Mercedes and reached under the front bumper. A key appeared in his hand and the locks popped.

"In, quickly."

Anne buckled Naomi into a child's seat behind Daniel and climbed in beside him. Were they adding car theft to the list of laws they had broken? She leaned her head back and sighed.

"What?"

"Naomi and I have to go to the bathroom."

"As soon as we get out of the city."

"Where are we going?"

"The harbor."

"Why aren't we staying here?"

"It may not be secure. If the list of safe houses were compromised and someone is following us, he will go to Montpellier and then here. There's a boat waiting for us. Maybe."

Maybe. Was his plan unraveling so fast?

She thought the harbor belonged to Perpignan, but they drove along the coast to Sante-Marie, Pyrenees-Orientales, a village of three thousand tucked between the mountains and the sea.

"Flat." Daniel murmured.

"Flat?"

"Not much cover. I need to see who's waiting for us."

"Someone's supposed to be here?"

"A boat, to take us to Israel. But I'm not sure any more, about my contacts."

He wasn't sure. Her chest tightened again. She'd have to stop reacting like this to everything he said, every setback. Always have a plan B he said.

He parked near the marina.

"There are field glasses in the console. Get in the driver's seat, watch me and if you see me raise my left arm, drive."

"Where?"

"Italy."

Drive to Italy, by herself with a small child.

"I—"

"Yes, you can."

He swung out of the car and she climbed over the shift into the driver's seat, pulled out the glasses and trained them on Daniel. He hid his blond hair under a floppy old man's hat, bent his shoulders and shuffled along beside the boats. Halfway, he dropped, put out one hand to balance and then, steadied, tied a shoelace.

A man on the deck of a nearby black cruiser tied where the two legs of the marina met, called out to Daniel. Daniel waved his hand, dismissively, Anne thought, and walked back towards the parking lot. He stumbled once, but recovered without falling.

Clever, Anne thought. If she didn't know better, she would be sure he was an old man in the early stages of Parkinson's.

She shifted into the passenger seat when he opened the door.

"What?"

"When we're out of here."

He crossed the causeway back to the village. Two roundabouts later, he drove onto the D-81. The D roads, Anne remembered from a long-ago trip with her husband Michael, were county roads, lots of exits, but liable to be slow.

"Where are we going?"

"Limoux."

"What went wrong?"

"The man on the boat."

"Because he shouted at you?"

"Because he wasn't the right guy."

"So little."

"Yes. I know him and I don't trust him."

The landscape changed and soon they were driving through low, rocky mountains along a less-travelled road. Vineyards climbing the slopes alternated with deep gorges. Anne turned her back to the window.

"Are you afraid of heights?"

"Yes."

"We have an hour and a half to go but we'll stop in Estagel."

"What mountains are these?"

"The Pyrenees Orientales."

Anne fought down her panic to enjoy their beauty.

A castle of stone, growing from the summit of a rocky crag, loomed against the sky and marked the village of Estagel.

"That castle is called Queribus," Daniel said. "This is the country of the Cathars."

"Cathars?"

"An heretical Christian sect that was wiped out in the 14th Century. They believed in the dualistic nature of God, with an evil Devil who created the physical world and a good God who created heaven and angels. Reincarnation played a role in their beliefs as well. They were persecuted and destroyed by the Catholic Church."

"A common historical theme."

"Yes."

They parked near the square and Anne took Naomi to bathroom while Daniel ordered lunch.

"What about staying there?" She pointed across the plaza to a small inn.

"No, I need the supplies from the next house. You're limping. Why?"

"Just a bruise on my left leg."

Daniel chose a table at the wall of the cafe, where he could watch, Anne thought. Adam, in Vermont did the same, and Thomas. So, in fact, did Winston.

Perhaps he was one of them, too? Spooks or spies or cops. Perhaps she should make her way to the Israeli embassy—"

"Elizabeth."

She jumped, overturning a glass of water and bringing a waiter with a white towel.

She'd forgotten she was Elizabeth.

"I'm sorry. I was daydreaming."

"Are you ready to go?"

"Yes." No, not really, but what choice did she have. She bundled Naomi out of her chair and Daniel carried her back to the van.

"Pay attention," he said. "You need to watch for them with me."

"Who?"

"Esti and Sergio. One or both."

"Esti? I thought she was a baby-sitter?"

"No. She's the boss and she's relentless."

"How did your people not know this before?"

"We think the mole buried the information. Trust no one. No one except me."

And Thomas, she thought. If Thomas were to come, she would trust him.

* * *

Sergio followed the GPS to an industrial street on the outskirts of Montpellier, a city of more than five hundred thousand.

Loading docks interrupted the facade of the rusted metal-clad building at number 3572, the entrance further down the street locked and barred.

He swore and pulled out his phone.

"Whom are you calling?" Esti complained about this

woman, said she was too controlling.

"Colette?"

"Yes."

"Sergio, from Setenil. I'm at the safe-house in Montpellier. The address is a closed factory."

"Give me a few minutes. I will check the information."

He retraced his steps to the van and dialled another number.

"Mama?"

"*Si.*"

He listened to her talk about her health and the garden and his nieces and nephews.

"And you, my son. Are you well? Do you have a relationship with God?"

Again, God. He sighed and brought the phone back up to his ear.

"I think it might be time to come home."

"Are you sick?"

"Sick of my job." At that moment, the pips indicating an incoming call sounded.

"I have to go. I love you, Mama."

He answered the call.

"Sergio, the information we gave you was corrupted. We think you must go to Perpignan."

CHAPTER 15

Daniel followed the D-117 to the town of Caudies de Fenouilledes. Ahead of them, traffic slowed and then stopped. Men stood outside their cars, gesticulating and yelling. Daniel turned right into a street signed Grand Rue, and parked. A knot of young teens loitered on the sidewalk, one of them tossing a soccer ball into the air.

"I'm going to find out what's ahead. Stay in the car."

Little traffic moved on Grand Rue, a narrow street of grey-stoned buildings with clay-tile roofs and bright-blue shutters, some with jaunty baskets of red geraniums hanging beneath. Daniel strolled to the line of waiting cars, and talked to one of the men. After a time, they shook hands and Daniel ambled back, pausing to light a cigarette. He took a few puffs, and then ground the cigarette under his heel. He pocketed the butt before climbing back into the car.

"And?"

"Police roadblock up ahead on D-117. We'll take the D-9."

"For us?"

"The guy I was talking to didn't know what had happened up ahead. We have to assume they're searching for us."

"You mean for me?"

"For us, Anne. How long will they take to find the guy in the red Fiat who passed us on the way out of Setenil? We're in this together."

"Why didn't we go to the police in Barcelona and explain to them what had happened?"

"They would have arrested both of us, and returned the child to Esti."

"I think Thomas was driving that car."

"Wishful thinking. No one told me anything about him coming to Spain, and his bosses would have told mine."

"What if he came on his own? I need to call him."

"No. First we'll get out of this town."

At the intersection, behind the sign for D-9 stood a medieval building, half-timbered, the upper story partially-bricked in a herringbone pattern, the pale green doors so short a man as tall as Daniel would duck, set in a ground level built of ancient stone. How she wanted to escape inside and hide.

Daniel turned right and soon they left the town behind. Fields, checker-boarded in grey and green lay on both sides.

"Are we done with mountains?" she asked.

"Not yet." He pointed ahead to wooded foothills that rose to meet the rocky crags and beyond them the snow-capped Pyrenees.

Mountains, again.

"What if they blocked the road along here, too?"

"Perhaps it wasn't for us."

A few kilometers later, the road climbed between hills of white-streaked grey rock, a few trees clinging to the scant earth in the crevasses. All that stood between them and a precipitous drop into the deep valley were low concrete blocks. Anne turned her back and closed her eyes.

"Anne. Don't go to sleep. I need you to watch."

"We're the only ones on the road."

"A motorcycle's behind us. Sergio or Esti may take this route too."

The road narrowed, winding through the rock-cuts. Northern Ontario, she thought, an empty land with the bones exposed.

"Have you used a gun since Bermuda?"

"Of course not. Why?"

"I want you to be familiar with the one in the glove box. It isn't loaded yet."

"I don't like guns, Daniel. I won't shoot anyone, so what's the point."

"Perhaps to save Naomi's life, or your own."

Her own. She'd fired a gun in Bermuda to save herself, even if the shot had gone wild and instead, he killed the man who hunted her.

She the gun from the glove-box and sat with it in her lap.

"Keep it holstered," he said. "It's ready when you take it out."

"And the safety?"

"In the trigger. Pull back on the barrel to load the chamber, and then pull back on both parts of the trigger. Aim for the body mass."

"Daniel, I—"

"Now you know. Keep your eyes on the mirror."

In the distance, climbing the hill behind them, a dark, red-helmeted figure astride a silver motorcycle followed.

"How long to Limoux?"

"Another three-quarters of an hour."

* * *

An hour later, after driving through heavily-forested hills overlooking the river Aude, Anne and Daniel arrived in Limoux. The motorcyclist waved to them as he passed and took the D-620. Daniel continued on the D-188 until they left the town behind. Anne read on in her guidebook, about the 14th century wars and 16th Century plague and the influence of Catharism. Catholicism returned to the town by the 16th Century, bringing a thirty-year war between the Catholics and the Calvinists. Eglise St. Jacques housed a piano museum. Why a piano museum? Unique in France it said, but nothing about its history. Louis XIII reestablished royal control in 1642. The French Revolution passed with no violence locally.

"How big is this town?"

"About ten thousand people. The French *Maquis* and the American OSS operated around here in the Second World War."

"Too small. We'll stand out."

"Yes, but we're a Canadian couple with their grandchild, here to vacation for a month."

"What?" He glanced at her and back at the road in time to evade an oncoming truck.

"When I go to the nearest store, I'll tell people while I shop for milk and bread. We can hide in plain sight."

"No."

"Why not?"

"It doesn't work, no matter what you have seen on

117

television or at the movies. Someone always talks." He pulled off the road and parked.

"If they have the wrong information—"

"It doesn't work." He sighed and turned in his seat towards her. "We're running from people skilled in tradecraft. They're looking for the basics—a woman who speaks English, a child, probably a man, new to the district, renting a house from an absentee landlord. This place is too small."

Daniel drove down a track rutted by some heavy vehicle. A tractor, Anne supposed. They stopped in front of a stone cottage or barn or...a cow byre. The old word from home came unbidden into Anne's thoughts. Her chest tightened and a thick lump rose into her throat. Home.

"Where are we?" she said, her voice pinched from the effort of forcing the words past the lump.

"Safe." He leaned back in his seat and passed a hand over his face.

Safe. He said they were safe in Barcelona until they weren't.

Naomi stirred and rubbed her eyes.

"I'm hungry."

"I know you are, Dolly. We'll eat as soon as we go inside. What about food?" she said to Daniel.

"Supplies in the house."

No cows inside, just raw stone walls that oozed cold. Daniel lit a fire in a black cast iron stove at one end of the long room. Behind the stove, the wall was papered in winding blue clematis. Anne unpacked the food and gave Naomi a sandwich of bread and cheese. A wooden table, its surface showing tool marks and black circles from long-ago pots, stood near the stove. She tucked

Naomi into an armchair that squatted where it would receive the most heat.

"Is this Israel?" Naomi said.

"No, a country called France. We're still a long way from Israel but Daniel's taking us as fast as he can, so we have to be patient."

"Come here," Daniel said. "I want to show you something." He was standing beside the stove, running his hand down the wall, his long fingers pressing on each flower.

"What are you doing?"

"Push on this area of the wall, if you need to hide." His fingers brushed a flower directly behind the stovepipe.

The section moved forward, revealing a cavity behind, big enough for her and Naomi.

"And you?"

"I won't be hiding. Keep Naomi safe until I come for you."

"If you don't come?"

"Listen. When you haven't heard anything for a time or you hear a vehicle leave, come out."

"And then."

"Go to this address in Menton."

Alone. He meant she go on alone. The lump in her throat grew larger. Daniel was still talking. She strained to listen past her fear.

"If Menton is compromised, move on to this address in Italy."

"Italy?" She tucked the paper in the pocket of her jeans.

"Yes. An old Jewish woman lives there. Old, very clever. Off the grid. No one should be able to follow you because she's on no one's list but mine. Her name is Sarah."

"Yes, if I have to go on alone." She had to get out of the dank cottage, into the sun. "We're going to walk in the garden for a few minutes."

"And we'll leave."

"If we must."

CHAPTER 16

Surrealist painter Salvador Dali declared Perpignan's railway station to be the center of the universe but Sergio wanted to find the woman and the child, get the job done and leave. He left his car in a street near the train station and walked the two blocks to the address of the safe house

A time-scarred oak door blocked the way into the apartment. A few moments work on the lock and he entered the courtyard, looking for a ground floor apartment. An elderly lady watched him from a balcony on the first floor. He waved to her and strode to the door on the left. Why the fuck hadn't they told him which ground-floor apartment?

The name on the door matched his information and he searched inside for evidence of the woman and child. Unused towels, unopened bottles of milk in the refrigerator and uncut loaves of bread on the counter, no trash in the bin: nothing indicated a visitor.

He left, miming locking the door behind him for the benefit of the curious woman on the balcony. He waved again.

In the car, he called Esti.

"I'm in Perpignan and there's no one here and no one's been here. What next?"

"Why call me? I thought you were getting orders direct from Switzerland now?"

"Fuck off, Esti. I was pissed that they sent me to a boarded-up factory in Montpellier and I wanted to be sure she knew it. The woman's ahead of me. Where?"

"I'll call and get back to you."

He drove away from the center of town and stopped near a cafe with three tables lined up under scarlet geraniums cascading from a window box. He sat down, ordered wine and tapas of sardines on toasted bread. A geranium leaf tickled his cheek and he broke it off, crushing it between his fingers. The peppery scent took him to his grandmother's garden in her villa in Madrid and the summer he spent with her when his mother was ill. Mass every day. But he played where he liked and ate his grandmother's good food and stayed up with the adults until 10 p.m.. He remembered holding her hand, smaller than his even when he was a child, while they walked up the steps into the church.

His phone interrupted his memories.

"The next house is in Limoux. I will text you the address."

"No change in the orders?"

"What change do you expect?"

"The child—"

"The child, too."

"But—"

"The child also or you will be next. Do you understand?"

"Yes." He cut off her next sentence. Perhaps he would take the child to his mother and tell her she was his.

He took the D-117 exit from the E-15 towards Estagel.

* * *

122

Anne and Naomi, hand-in-hand, wandered away from the house into an impressionist landscape of scarlet and yellow flowers blooming in the sunny intervals between plane trees. She was still limping. Daniel turned away when his phone buzzed.

"We have information for you," the familiar voice on the phone said.

"Yes."

"The houses—you know their quality— may have lost some of that."

They always spoke in riddles. The quality was security.

"And the cause?"

"Here, we think. An investigation continues."

"My choices?"

"Only one."

They meant leave again because of a leak. How long could he keep the child on the run without attracting attention from the police?

"How long?"

"Unknown." Unknown, and him with a child and a woman whose only thought was for the child's welfare. She didn't understand the relentless forces against them.

When Anne and Naomi returned, he told Anne they would have to leave.

"She has to sleep, Daniel, at least for a few hours and she needs to eat."

"One hour, no more."

CHAPTER 17

Sergio stopped at the intersection, behind the column of vehicles waiting to be processed by the police.

"What's up?" he asked another motorcyclist idling ahead of him.

"Roadblock. They're are looking for some drug dealer."

"Are you from around here? Is there another way to Limoux?"

"Sure, go right and take D-9

Sergio replaced his helmet, revved his engine, and turned right.

The D-9 switchbacked through the mountains. Sergio opened up and roared up the highway, around the S-curves, leaning into the hills. A van appeared on the road ahead of him. The switchback made it appear that the van was coming towards him, but in a moment it disappeared from view.

No houses or even farms broke the endless trees and rock. The D-9 became the D-109 and then the D-118 for the final run to the town. At the junction he passed the van and waved to driver. Tourists, he thought, camping around France on their big holiday from England. He hated the English. They lived like aristocrats all over his country, buying the pubs and pushing up the prices for houses. His brothers couldn't buy houses in their own village.

Esti wanted him to get this done fast, but he needed to sleep and eat. In Limoux, he found a Fasthotel, took a room and slept for an hour, showered and ate in the cafe. He checked his phone for the address and the map. It would soon be over and he would go home.

* * *

Anne roused Naomi from her nap, brushed her unruly curls and tied them up with navy ribbons. They sat at the scarred pine table and Naomi ate a sandwich, first taking off the top piece of bread and inspecting the contents before she took a careful bite. Daniel stood at the door, keeping watch.

"We have to go soon," he said, turning to her.

"We'll be ready as soon as she goes to the bathroom. You moved the car?"

"Yes, to a derelict building beyond the woods. The spare keys are on the front passenger-side tire. The weapon is in the glove-box."

Anne closed her fists and willed her throat to stay open. " I don't know if I could do it. It took everything I had last time to fire. I might not be able to kill someone to save my own life, not again."

"To save Naomi, not yourself." He grabbed her shoulders and stared into her eyes. "To save a child. That's who you are."

Naomi tugged at her arm.

"*Safta*, I want to wash my hands."

"Yes. Come with me."

The sink was too high for her to reach but Anne

lifted her and held her while she washed each finger. A window, with a view of the woods beside the house, opened over the sink. A movement caught her eye. She put Naomi on the floor and handed her a towel, all the time keeping her gaze on the trees. And then she saw him, a man, lurking at the edge. Sergio.

"Daniel, he's here."

"Hide."

She picked up Naomi and pushed the section of wall beside the stove, tucked Naomi inside and closed the door behind them. Blackness pressed down on her. They would have to stay in this dank hole until Daniel came for them.

"*Safta* — "

"Shss. We have to hide and be very quiet or Sergio will find us."

"I don't like Sergio."

"I don't either. Be very still."

Anne clutched Naomi to her, beating down her claustrophobic fear of enclosed spaces. The fetid smell reminded her of escaping through the tunnel in Bermuda, steps ahead of the last hired killer who had followed her. After this, she would stay home. No more intrigue. And no more Thomas. She strained to hear something, anything from outside, but there was only silence. Naomi wrapped her arms around Anne's neck and Anne hugged her close.

* * *

Sergio ran across the narrow lawn to the side of the house and waited. The cold of the old stones leaked into his back where he pressed against the wall. He strained to hear. Nothing. No child's voice, or woman's either. Perhaps they'd left, moving on to whatever safe house came next.

He edged around the corner, glanced at the front of the farmhouse, and backed away. A man, standing in the doorway. They thought she had help. The stranger would be *Mossad* and dangerous.

He waited. Nothing.

He crept back along the wall, peering through the dirty windows as he went. No sign of the woman or the child. What had he done with them? He couldn't kill him before he knew.

He made it back to the corner nearest the door where the *Mossad* agent waited, took another look, and ducked back. The agent concentrated on the woods to the right. He stepped out, the agent swung round and shot.

An explosion of pain in his left arm jolted him back. He fired and the agent crumpled in the doorway. Sergio grabbed at a window frame for support, fighting off nausea and dizziness. He edged along the wall, glanced around the door frame. No one else. The *Mossad* agent lay with his shooting arm outstretched, still gripping his weapon. He tried his neck for a pulse. Nothing, or so weak it didn't matter. The wound in the agent's belly oozed blood. Gut-shot.

He leaned back against the wall, pressing his shirt sleeve into the wound in his arm. Odd, no pain now, just the warmth of the blood oozing through the shirt and the smell, like his grandmother's ancient copper kettle. He slumped to the ground beside the body, waiting for dizziness to clear. A few minutes he stood up, clutching the wall. Fuck. Now he would have to call for help again. Where would he have sent the woman? Maybe they were hidden in the house.

He stumbled through the two rooms but found nothing. They likely scrambled to put distance between them and the house. He drank at the sink and then, outside, searched the ground. Footprints led out to the garden and back again and then nothing except the tire tracks in front of the house. The driver would hit pavement in a hundred meters. Where would she take the child?

He sat on the steps beside the agent's body and called Esti. The blood from the corpse pooled beside him, a gel the color of *Sangre de Toro* wine, of the stains in the bullring in Ronda. The blood smell made him gag. Some of it came from the wound in his left arm. Not so much pain. Not the bone.

"They're gone."

"Did you see them?"

"No. I shot the agent. The woman and child are on their own."

"Stupid. He knew where they were going." He pounded the phone against his thigh before he answered.

"Next time, you do it."

"I will call you the location of the next safe house. In the meantime, get out of there. Now."

He didn't tell her the agent had shot him too. If she came, he'd have no chance to take the child to his mother. He'd drive the D-118 north to the A-61 at Carcassonne and east to Narbonne. He would wait on the beach for her to call him.

* * *

Hours passed or so it seemed. Anne cuddled Naomi, rocking her until the child's breathing slowed and she slept.

Anne brought up images, peaceful ones of sand and sea and sky but that triggered memories of Bermuda and a young man's dying eyes. She tried again, this time pictures of her garden in high summer: pink roses clambering up the grey stone of her house; stands of pink and peach and yellow snapdragons in the south-facing beds; cool green and white and wrinkled blue hostas on the north side. She lay back in a *Muskoka* chair while the gulls swooped over the water. She stayed in that peaceful dream until Naomi stirred in her arms.

How long had it been? She checked her phone. Fifteen minutes, maybe less. No sounds other than their breathing. Naomi whimpered into the silence.

"*Safta*, I don't like it here."

Somewhere, a faint pop, and another.

"Neither do I. Did you hear anything outside?"

"Just some noises."

"What kind of noises?"

"The sounds the rifles make." Where had she heard rifles? But what did she know about an Israeli childhood. Fear made the shots echo in her mind.

"Have they stopped?"

"Yes."

"We must be quiet for a little longer."

Time ticked past on her phone. Another ten minutes.

She pushed open the door to their cramped space and ventured out. Still no sounds. As she came around the stove, she saw Daniel's body.

She ran to him, calling his name. She slipped in the pool of blood oozing from his wound, stumbled on the doorstep and fell to her knees beside him; her anxious fingers searched for a pulse in his neck. His blood was still flowing. His heart must be beating. She heard gasping and realized it was her own. She willed her breathing to slow, and tried his carotid again and found it, faint and rapid but steady.

She pulled his shirt open and out of his jeans and wadded the tail into the hole in his abdomen. Where was her phone? She dialled 112, the emergency number for the EU.

"What service?"

"Ambulance. A man has been shot."

"Where."

"Limoux." What was the address? She'd seen it, written on the information left on the table by the owners.

"The address?"

"A farm off the D-118 towards Carcassonne, the next lane to the left past the road to Galerie El Indalo."

"I have dispatched ambulance and police. Stay on the line, please."

"Hurry. The wound is in his abdomen and he's bleeding. My phone is dying."

She turned it off, and felt once more for Daniel's pulse. His eyes opened.

"Leave," he whispered, raising one hand to touch her sleeve.

"I can't leave you."

"You must. Go. I'll live, or I won't. Go." His eyes closed.

"*Safta*, is he dead?" Naomi's tear-stained face looked up at her.

"No. We must go."

* * *

The agent waited in the commander's office. The grey walls, metal desk, small windows overlooking a parking lot reminded him of why he worked for Interpol and not the police force in the Andalusian village where he'd started. Where was this commander? Lunch, the clerk said. A long lunch.

The door opened, and the commander, in his starched green uniform, polished boots and holster, strode in, his right hand outstretched, the other holding the agent's card.

"A pleasure to meet a fellow police officer. What is Interpol doing in this tiny village?"

The agent ignored the hand and said, "Sit down, Commander. I have to discuss the matter of fraudulent arrest warrants with you."

"Fraudulent?" A bead of sweat appeared on his upper lip, in a gap in his moustache. It rolled down over his upper lip and a nervous tongue flicked it away.

"Yes." He handed over the bulletin on Anne.

"We have reason to believe this was issued only for the purpose of tracking this woman. Who has induced you to do this?"

"I have a sworn—"

"Do not try my patience." The agent loomed over the desk. "Who? And I warn you, your answer must be truthful or I will arrest you."

"You have no—"

The agent slammed his hand on the desk. The sound echoed through the tiny space.

"Who?" he whispered.

"A *Basque* woman and her boyfriend. They insist the woman stole some identity papers from them."

"Withdraw the bulletin."

"I…that's not possible."

"Now."

The commander buzzed his clerk and gave the order.

"What now?" he asked the agent.

"Now, I'm leaving, but not forgetting. I'll be back if I find something has happened to the woman."

When he turned back at the door, the commander had his head on the desk, shoulders heaving.

What a coward, he thought. Outside the building, he dialled Lyon.

"Boss, it's done."

CHAPTER 18

Anne ran into the house, grabbed her backpack and Naomi's, strapped them on and ran with her to the protection of the woods. The claxon of the ambulance sounded behind her. Ahead of her a rudimentary trail wound through the trees, half-filled in by underbrush. She picked Naomi up and disappeared, she hoped, from view of the police cars and ambulance that entered the lane.

She followed the trail across the woods. She stumbled on deadfall, gasped at the pain in her leg, clutched at a tree branch to right herself and kept going. The whole alien forest worked to prevent her escape. Boulders cropped up in her path and shrubs with needle-sharp thorns dug at her legs. Ahead, a meadow glowed in the sunshine. Hidden from view by the last of the forest, the derelict building Daniel had told her about stood in the field. She'd pictured a frame shack, but that was an image from home. The stone building, battered perhaps by the elements or war, stood in the clearing at the end of a lane overgrown with weeds and bushes. In the distance the sirens pulsed and echoed.

When she got closer, she saw bullet-ridden walls and a pockmarked door fastened to the casing by a solitary hinge. Inside, she found the car and the keys. She put Naomi into her car seat, and only then noticed a note on the driver's side.

> *Anne,*
>
> *If you find this, you are alone and have to save Naomi by yourself. Go to the address in Menton, but be careful when you approach the house. Remember the weapon in the glove box. Pull the trigger and the safety switch built into it, together to fire.*
> *Remember Italy.*

Her chest ached. Daniel was dying because she wouldn't leave. How important had it been to walk in the meadow? Why had she wasted so much time?

She reached across and took out the gun. In Bermuda, she fired at a voice in the dark. Could she kill someone to save Naomi and herself? She would face Esti or Sergio or both, alone. Would she have the courage?

The gun, heavy and smooth, weighed on her hands, dragging them down onto her thighs. She inserted the cartridge with the bullets as Daniel had shown her. The safety was on, he said.

The rearview mirror reflected Naomi's face, just emerging from babyhood, innocent and trusting. She adjusted the mirror, away from Naomi's face and caught a glimpse of her own eyes, pupils dilated in fear. To save Naomi, she would do what she must. She put the gun back, set the GPS for Menton and drove.

His sudden halt confused a woman leading another troop of children and they bunched up behind her.

"Complications? Why haven't you brought her home?" Steel, forged in military and political campaigns, reinforced the anger in his demand.

"We had to get her out of Spain. We think we have a mole in the organization; our agent was compromised. The woman he recruited to work with him fled with the child."

The children's minder behind them clucked her annoyance.

"Find them," he said, oblivious to children moving around them, like a stream divided by a granite boulder.

"Our agent lies unconscious in a French hospital. The woman may be on her way to the next safe house whose location the mole betrayed. We should walk on; people are noticing."

"No statements."

"But your granddaughter?"

"They will kill her." His voice broke and he hesitated, getting control before he went on, "and the woman, whatever I say now. Tell them they must wait for the vote and if there is no proof of life—"

"Are you sure? Her parents?"

Her parents, his daughter would never forgive him, never.

"They trust me to do what is right for Naomi and for Israel."

* * *

The next morning, Esti sat in the living room of her house in Setenil, cleaning her weapons. It was time to call that Swiss bitch again. How she hated her disembodied voice, its careful syllables and accusing tone. She dialled.

"Yes."

Esti ground her teeth, and then answered. "The *Mossad* agent is dead; the woman and child, gone."

"And Sergio?"

"Awaiting instructions. Where is the next safe house?"

"The woman may choose to go elsewhere, if she is on her own."

"She may not be. Another man here, a stranger, talked to Caldwell. He too has disappeared."

"And Caldwell?"

"I haven't seen him today."

"They are not pleased."

Esti fought down the impulse to heave the phone through the nearest window, counted a slow ten and answered. "So?"

"The next house is in Menton. Go yourself to meet Sergio. Leave tomorrow. They want you to stay in Setenil for one more day, to keep up the illusion of the distraught nanny. Afterwards, there will be instructions for you."

"And the grandfather in Israel?"

"Not your concern. Await instructions."

She rubbed the barrel of her favorite weapon, until her breathing slowed and her heart stopped racing.

Later, Esti called Sergio again.

"The next safe house is in Menton, near the border with Italy."

A knock came at her door. The commander stood on her doorstep.

"What are you doing here?"

"We need to talk."

Esti leaned back against the doorpost of her villa, a pose that thrust her breasts towards him, brushing his arm as the commander moved past her.

"I've had a visit from Interpol," he said, swinging around to confront her.

He wasn't taller, but heavier than she was. His stomach bulged over his belt and jowls drooped from his jaw line.

"And?"

"And he threatened me. I withdrew the bulletin."

"Fool." She slapped his face, leaving a red welt under his left eye. "Did you tell him about me?"

"No, but unless you make it worth my while, I will." He grabbed her wrists and pulled her against his chest.

"I'll have to change into something special," she whispered. "Why don't you get more comfortable, too."

He released her wrists and his tongue licked his bottom lip. She undid the first three buttons on his shirt. He unbuckled his holster and dropped it on the sofa behind him. His hands ran down her back and across her buttocks, searching between her legs.

"Give me a moment." She slipped away and up the stairs.

In the bathroom, she shrugged out of her jeans and into a red gown that covered her from neck to ankles, closed down the front with tiny ivory buttons. She chose her favorite derringer from a collection of weapons behind a stone in the wall of her bedroom, and tucked it, safety off, into the pocket of the gown.

He'd unbuttoned his shirt to his navel. His abdomen, vast and pale beneath a furry blanket of black hair, jutted into her as he wrapped his arms around her. She caressed his back. He panted and his left hand reached for her breast. She took the derringer from her pocket, brought her arm up around him and fired into the base of his neck.

His eyes bulged and he whispered no before crumpling at her feet. No blood, but she couldn't have everything. With the sudden release of tension killing gave her, her heart retrieved its normal pace, her breathing slowed, her erect nipples retracted. The fools always thought they were arousing her, but only the prospect of killing them, of watching the light go out, excited her.

She cleaned all trace of herself from the villa, removed her long dark wig and brushed her short blonde curls. The clothes she wore as Esti, the nanny, went into a green plastic bag, to be dropped off at a trash collection site far from Setenil.

His body sprawled on the carpet, his cargo pants gathered around his knees. She lifted one of his arms with the toe of her boot and let it fall.

Outside, she carried the bag to her waiting car, and drove away, free of the appalling village. Tomorrow, or the next day, she would be in Menton.

CHAPTER 20

The GPS directed Anne around the little city of Narbonne to the A-9. Before Nimes, she left the motorway at the junction with A-54. She crossed over the broad brown expanse of the Rhone as she passed through the town of Arles. She would have like to stop here. She noticed signs for a Nature Reserve and Roman ruins and the sea was close. Vincent van Gogh painted here—a work called Starry Night over the Rhone, a beautiful night sky with haloed stars reflected in the dark water—and hundreds of other paintings and sketches. Allied bombing of Arles in World War II destroyed the house where he painted his Yellow Room.

But they needed sleep and food. She took an off-ramp when she cleared the suburbs of the city, following a sign for a countryside hotel. She drove past fields of lavender and sunflowers, radiant purple and saffron in the evening sun, on a road that passed through an arch of Sycamores. Everywhere the landscape was familiar from the paintings of the Impressionists.

Another sign indicated the turn to a gravel lane, its center choked with weeds, erosion reducing it to barely enough room for one vehicle, led to a sprawling stone and brick bungalow. A German Shepherd, its ribs showing beneath a shaggy coat, growled and barked at the car as Anne stopped on the drive in front of the building. Not too promising, she thought, taking in the shed attached by what looked to be two nails to the end of the house, and a few rangy geraniums struggling in window-boxes.

She tapped on her horn but that only drove the dog to more frenzied barking. She waited. No one emerged from the building. She sat on the horn again.

A thin, almost wasted man, walked up from the barn and bellowed at the dog. He slunk away, his tail firmly between his legs. Anne rolled down her window.

"Yes, Madame."

"Do you have a room free for tonight?"

"Yes."

"Could I see it please?"

The front door, scratched and ripped at the bottom—from the dog, Anne presumed—opened to a narrow foyer with a hallway leading off to the left. Anne followed, past two doors to a room at the end.

The dark room, furnished with two beds and a dresser scarred with cigarette burns and white rings from wet glasses, smelled of smoke and dog and old clothes. But the bathroom was spotless and the linen on the beds, clean.

"And the cost?"

"Fifty euros."

"Fine. We will stay one night. Do you provide breakfast?"

"Seven a.m.—9 a.m."

"And where is the breakfast room?"

"Down here."

She followed him back down the dank corridor.

"Register here." He pointed to a desk in one corner of a room furnished with three tables covered in yellow cloths. Thin sunlight struggled through one dusty window. A pale woman, equally as thin as the man, her black hair tied in a loose bun, drew back as they approached.

"One night," he said and tromped off.

"Passports, Madame. For you and the child. Is she your child, Madame? She does not look like you."

Suspicion poured from this woman, Anne thought, and felt her heart race.

The woman reached one red, rough-skinned hand out to stroke Naomi's auburn curls.

"My granddaughter." Anne tucked Naomi under one arm.

"You have letters for the child?"

Odd, Anne thought. So particular about the legalities when they needed money so badly, or she presumed they did.

"Yes."

The woman wrote down the information on the passports and the letter of permission in a black ledger.

"Who is this lady?" she asked Naomi, who clung to Anne's leg.

"*Safta* Elizabeth." Naomi said.

"What?"

"She is my granddaughter. I'm taking her to Italy to visit her aunt and then home to Israel. She's tired. We've driven too many miles today and she needs a nap in a bed, certainly not questions."

"Ah."

The woman tapped her pen on the ledger and closed it with a snap.

141

"How will you pay?"

"Cash."

After she had paid, Anne picked Naomi up and carried her back down the hall to their room. From the door she glimpsed the woman with her phone to her ear. Reporting them, Anne thought. She hustled Naomi into the room and locked it behind them.

CHAPTER 21

Day Twelve

Esti told her phone to call the number in Switzerland. She wasn't supposed to have it programmed in, but they couldn't have everything their way. Always keep a record of contacts. Her own rule. Her phone recorded her calls. The woman in Switzerland answered.

"What is it, Esti? You are early."

Her schedule, always. One day she would quit the job and kill this woman. "I'm leaving this village. Now."

She watched the few cars travelling in the same direction, towards Ronda. No sirens. They'd miss him soon, but perhaps he didn't tell his staff where he went. No, of course he didn't. The landlord wouldn't come until the rent was due in two days. But someone, in the plaza or in the neighborhood would tell the cops no one had seen her. She needed to put distance between herself and Setenil. Colette was jabbering again.

"Esti? I said they want you to stay another day."

"I can't. I killed the commander."

Silence. Why didn't she say something? All she ever did was put her on hold and speak to the boss, and give orders in her prissy voice.

She passed Acinipo and took the main road towards Ronda and the coast. Construction, as always. Would they never be done? She halted at the stop sign held by a woman in a reflective jacket. What a job. Tied to one place, the only duty to turn her sign from stop to slow and back again. She would die first.

"They want you to leave for Menton. I am sending the address to you again. Later, they will require an explanation."

"He tried to rape me. Is that explanation enough?"

"That will depend. Call in twelve hours."

Esti threw her phone to the passenger seat, checked her rearview—still no cops. The flag-woman turned the sign from stop to slow and she shot forward. What did she mean—that will depend? The last job for them, no matter what they paid. The last job.

* * *

Anne woke early, before sunrise. Naomi slept, one arm curled around her donkey, the other tucked under her chin. Anne sat beside her and patted her back.

"Come, Naomi. We'll eat our breakfast and drive to the place Daniel told me about."

"I'm too tired and I don't want to drive any more."

"I know, Sweetpea. I don't want to drive anymore either but we have to go, so I can call your mommy and daddy to come for you."

"I don't like it in the back all by myself."

"The carseat only goes in the back. Bring your donkey and we'll get something to eat." She reached for Naomi's hand but she gripped her donkey with both hands, stuck out her lower lip and shook her head.

"Yes. We must go." She picked Naomi up and carried her to the breakfast room.

The sullen woman from the night before brought tepid *cafe-au-lait* to her and some warm juice for Naomi. The croissants tasted like rubber and the butter rancid.

"Do you have anything fresher?" she asked.

The sullen woman muttered "*Merde*" and stomped away.

Anne scooped up Naomi, left the breakfast room and limped across the parking lot to her car.

"Why are we going?" Naomi said.

"The lady brought us bad food."

"Why?"

"I don't know. We'll find a better place to eat."

If they didn't stop for long, they should be in Menton in two hours.

The night before, after she'd checked them in, the woman phoned someone. What if she'd been suspicious and called the police? The sooner they reached the safe house, the better. Now she understood the pressure Daniel felt to keep moving, stop as little as possible and stay in one place just long enough to eat and sleep.

A marked police car passed her, and another. What would she do at a roadblock? She needed to calm herself. She took long, deep breaths and concentrated on the road ahead. The police vehicles had disappeared.

At the next Aire de Service, a center for travellers on the A-8 she filled her car with gas and her child with food and rejoined the motorway for the final push to Menton.

* * *

In the afternoon, Sergio lay on the beach at Narbonne, his swollen left arm elevated on his backpack. The onshore breeze from the azure expanse of the Mediterranean dried the sweat gathering on his forehead. His fever wasn't dropping, in spite of the medication a pharmacist gave him. Why hadn't Esti called? He had to get to wherever the Canadian was going, kill her and take the child to his mother before Esti came looking for him.

He rolled up the sleeve of his shirt to expose his wound to the air. Yellow fluid that smelled like death soaked the bandages. He should change them but he couldn't, not by himself. He lay back and closed his eyes against the sun. His arm throbbed. Perhaps he should hit a pharmacy for some morphine, but that would slow him down too. When the phone rang, he rolled upright.

"Yes."

"Menton. I've sent you the address. Wait for me."

He didn't tell her about his arm. She'd say she'd do it and she would kill the child. He struggled to his feet, reached with his good arm for the pack and plodded back to his car. In the distance he could see the Massif de la Clape, pine forests in front of barren outcroppings of granite. His route took him away from the beach and the mountains, along the Mediterranean shore to the Italian border.

Esti didn't say where she was. Would she reach Menton before he did?

The traffic on the A-9 was thin, not like in the season, when the tourists clogged the freeways on their journey to the *Cote D'Azur.*

Within two hours he passed Nimes and drove into rain. The traffic slowed but he would arrive at Menton by nightfall.

* * *

Winston arrived in the plaza for his morning coffee. A knot of local people huddled around the cafe's owner. Puzzled tourists, fresh off the bus from Ronda, sat waiting while the staff listened to the boss.

"They found him in Esti's house," he heard someone say.

"Whom did they find?" Winston asked the closest person.

"The Guardia commander."

"What was he doing there?"

The person beside him shrugged, raised his eyebrows, and grimaced.

So it was like that, Winston thought. He moved to his table. The waiter hustled up, placed a cup in front of him and whispered, "The commander is dead."

"Dead? Heart attack?"

"No. Murdered. His trousers were around his knees and his gun and holster sat on the table. Esti is missing."

Missing. On the run, or after Anne. A pro, she'd continue on her mission.

"Did someone take her?" The waiter cast a glance towards his boss but he still chattered to the circle of curious villagers.

"They think she killed him."

"No! And the child?"

"Esti said the woman who sat with you every morning kidnapped her."

"Absurd."

The boss called the waiter who hurried away to the waiting tourists. Winston fingered his phone, wondering if he should call Thomas. This would make no difference, he decided. He would wait until or if Thomas called him. In the meantime, he dialled a number in Lyon. Henri answered.

"Henri, a fact from Setenil. The individual we spoke of is dead, murdered. Local gossip suggests the woman whose picture you have killed him. She is missing." His restless fingers drummed on the table.

"So. I'll issue an alert. We'll find her. A woman as beautiful as that is noticed."

"Thanks, Henri. If anything more happens here, I'll let you know."

He'd done what he could. Now Anne and her unknown friend were on their own. His fingers returned to their drumming and he thought of Anne, alone in the dark world of spies and intrigue. She'd been there before. Would she survive this time? A stab of pain shot through his chest. She must.

CHAPTER 22

The next morning Thomas waited in Barcelona, reading a newspaper and watching the few tourists take pictures of the square.

His phone vibrated on the table.

"Tom?" Quin's voice.

"Yes."

"The next safe house is in Perpignan. I e-mailed you the address."

"After Perpignan?"

"They won't tell me. Call me back if you don't find them and I'll get you the next one."

"That'll take too long."

"No way around it. They don't want to give up the safe house unless they need to."

"Thanks."

"One more thing, Tom. They think they have a mole; the list might be compromised."

"Damn. I'll call you from Perpignan."

He leaned forward on the bench, his hands gripped between his knees. He started this when he asked her to help in Bermuda and now she was on the run with only Ari between her and whoever had kidnapped the child in the first place. Ari had called in the favor he owed, not Anne, although Anne wouldn't see it that way.

Time to leave Barcelona and catch them in Perpignan, if they were still there. If they ever had been.

Two hours later, Thomas rang the bell at the oak door that barred the entrance to the apartment building. In a minute or two the door opened and an elderly woman, her hair pulled back in a chignon, a black scarf looped over a grey silk sweater, peered at him over glasses slid part way down her elegant nose.

He spoke to her in his fluent French, asking if she had seen the lady and child who rented the ground floor apartment number two.

"No, Monsieur. No one has been in that apartment at all this month, although the rent was paid."

"No one came at all?" Her job was to record who entered and left. A stranger would be an event.

"A man, yesterday. He had a key."

"Are you sure he had a key?"

"How else did he get in." She folded her arms across her chest and lifted her chin. The extra folds of skin quivered.

"Of course. Thank you."

He passed her a five euro note and turned to leave.

"One moment." She spoke to his back and he turned to face her.

"Yes."

"I didn't like the looks of him."

"Why? What didn't you like?"

"Young, dark, Spanish, furtive. He didn't ring at this door. Even the residents ring. It is only polite." Her upper lip, under its wisps of moustache, curled.

And no tip for her, Thomas thought.

"Thank you, Madame."

When he reached his car, he placed another call to Quin.

"Tom?"

"Yes. No one here in Perpignan, but I think Sergio is ahead of me."

"She hasn't called?"

"No."

"I'll get you the next address but it might take some time."

"Not too much time, Quin." Thomas rang off.

He wandered the streets of Perpignan while he waited. A rampart high above the city surrounded the castle of the Kings of Majorca. How, he wondered had a city in the mountains become capital of a nation named after an island. He rounded a corner into the *Place de la Republique*, its buildings painted in Mediterranean colors of peach and cream. A bar-restaurant ahead of him sported taupe and red umbrellas above tangerine tables. Anne would have loved this, he thought, listening to the voices around him: American tourists—somehow louder than everyone else, even if they tried—a function perhaps of size, musical accents of Spanish and Catalan, snippets of African French. Mostly Catalan, he realized after a few minutes. More a Catalan city than French. He waited through the evening for a call from Quin. By midnight, he'd checked into a bed and breakfast and slept.

* * *

Further along the motorway, a sign indicating construction diverted Anne to an off-ramp. She followed the signs and the GPS, trying to find her way back to the A-8. The route took her through the village of *Puget*

Sur Argens and then *Rocquebrune sur Argens*. The mass of red rock that gave the town its name rose to the south from a forest of pine trees.

They stopped again at a roadside cafe for lunch.

"*Safta*, can I play in the park," Naomi asked, wiggling down off her chair and pointing to a charming space furnished with benches and swings and an expanse of grass.

"One moment, and I'll come with you."

Anne pushed Naomi on a swing and ate ice cream and for a few moments, forgot to be frightened, forgot the pain in her leg, now an ever present throb, forgot about Esti coming for them. But the sun moved lower in the sky, the shadows lengthened and Naomi drooped on a bench beside her.

"Are you tired now?"

"Yes."

"I think we'll go on to the place that is waiting for us, the one Daniel told me about."

"Will *Ima* be there?"

"No, I'll have to call." Who was Ima, Anne wondered. She checked the translation app on her phone. *Mommy.* Naomi was asking for her mother.

By the time they reached the intersection of DN-7 and the A-8, five hours later, Naomi was asleep. The traffic, mostly commercial trucks of all sizes, was heavy going east. Soon they would be in Menton.

* * *

In Perpignan, Esti stopped at a green, vinyl-clad hotel on the south side of the town.

"Forty euros," the clerk said. "Cash."

Forty euros for a bed, a shower room with a drain in

the floor in front of the toilet, a window that didn't open and an air-conditioner that filled the room with tepid air. She needed a few hours sleep after the eleven hour drive from Setenil but first, she had to call the Swiss bitch.

"Where are you?" Colette's precise voice said.

"Perpignan. In a hotel."

"Why have you stopped?" Again the questions. What was she? A robot?

"It was rest or crash."

"The vote is in four days and the grandfather is asking for proof of life again. You must find them."

"After I sleep. I'm no good to you dead on the side of the Autoroute." And a headache, threatening since Malaga, sent bursts of pain into her left eye.

"Four hours, no more."

Four hours. She'd sleep as long as she needed to. Sergio wasn't incompetent. He'd get to the woman first and it would be all over. Would he kill the child or sell her on? If he'd sold her, she would kill him.

* * *

Esti merged with the A-9. Rain began, sheets of it, pouring onto her windows and puddling on the highway. Now she concentrated on a road packed with traffic. The truck ahead, a long semi, and the SUV behind that, travelled at the speed limit. Best to get around the semi into the faster lane. She pulled out to pass.

What the hell was he doing?

The semi curved towards her, the giant gold letters on the side of its trailer—*Lait*—filled her vision and the scream of metal on metal echoed in the car. She fought to get control; the back end of her car swung into the guard rail, another screech of metal and her head bounced off the window but the car responded and she drove ahead of the truck. She glanced in her rearview mirror. Almost in slow-motion the semi behind hit the guardrail and jackknifed. The trailer and its load slammed into it and milk, pouring from a rupture in its side, flooded the highway, a pool of glistening white. But she was still ahead.

She took the next off ramp and found a service station. The car door wouldn't open. She crawled across the gearshift to the passenger side. Out of the car, she inspected the damage. Not too bad. Driveable. A wave of dizziness made her lean against the hood. Someone, a man, was talking to her.

"Are you all right?" he said.

"An accident on the A-9. A semi brushed me and I hit the guardrail and I think my head."

"Your head's bleeding. You better come in and sit, have a coffee. I'll call the traffic police."

"No. Don't do that. I can still drive and I have to be in Menton tomorrow."

"Up to you, lady, but come and drink a coffee anyway."

She walked towards the cafe of the service station, its lights blurred by the rain. The lights whirled and disappeared.

Someone was shining a light in her eyes. She hit the arm away.

"Take it easy," someone said. "We're checking you for concussion."

"I'm all right." She must be in an ambulance. Were they moving? No. She could still get away.

"I have to go…"

When she woke up, she knew they were moving, en route to some hospital, she supposed. What had they done with her stuff, her cases with her guns?

"My belongings?" she said to the young woman sitting beside her.

"The guy at the service center locked up your car. He said you wanted to drive on with it."

"The keys?"

"Here." She showed Esti the keys.

"Where are you taking me?"

"To an ER to be checked over."

"What's the name of the service center?"

"He gave me the card, in case you didn't remember. I'll give everything to you at the ER."

Esti closed her eyes, waking again when the EMS wheeled her into the Emergency Center.

CHAPTER 23

Rain began an hour before Menton, the traffic slowed, and then stopped. Naomi stirred in her carseat but didn't waken. The line burped ahead, one or two car-lengths at a time. A cruiser blocked one lane, and on the other side, two uniformed police, wearing white capes and hats, one standing, his hand on his weapon, the other leaning down, talked to a driver. Anne pulled her documents from her backpack. She fought to control her breathing. She imagined being at the bedside of an ill child, willing herself to be calm for the sake of the parents, for the nurses.

When she reached the roadblock, she rolled her window down and waited until the Gendarme reached her.

"Your license and registration, Madame."

She handed over the Canadian license and International Drivers License Daniel had given her.

"You have a child here. Do you have papers for her?"

"Yes." She gave him Naomi's passport and the French copy of the letter of permission and Naomi's school record.

"Where are you taking her?"

"To Rome, to meet her parents."

"Lower the back window, please. Does she speak French?"

"No, English and Hebrew and a little Spanish."

He spoke to Naomi in English. Why would they have an English-speaking officer unless they were looking for her. What had the woman at the motel said about her?

"Who is the lady who is driving this car?"

Naomi clutched her donkey tighter. "*Safta* Elizabeth."

Oh, good girl, Anne thought. She remembered.

"Where are you going?"

"To a country called Italy. My *Ima* is waiting for me."

"Ima?" The officer raised an eyebrow at Anne.

"Mama," Anne said.

He stepped back, spoke to his partner, and walked to his vehicle. A few moments later he returned.

"Well?"

"The owner of the hotel where you stayed was suspicious. We must ask you to pull ahead and wait."

"She saw all the papers you did." Anne let anger creep into her voice.

"She was being a good citizen."

"Perhaps." Anne turned the key in the ignition, put the car in gear and drove ahead into a parking area. Or perhaps she wanted a bribe, Anne thought.

An hour passed. She took Naomi into the front seat with her.

"*Safta,* why are we not driving?"

"The man wants to talk to us but he's busy so we have to wait."

"I need to pee-pee."

Anne picked her up and carried her to the blockading police car.

"Yes, Madame?"

"My granddaughter needs a WC. Either let us go or direct us to your station so she can use the facilities."

He looked up from his tablet computer, startled perhaps by her tone.

"You are in no position to make demands."

"Not demands, requests. Or shall I sit quietly in my car and call the Canadian Embassy and tell them that I am being detained for no reason."

"I'm awaiting instructions."

"Ask again." She swung around and marched away.

"Are you angry, *Safta?*"

"Yes, Naomi. That man is unkind. Can you hold your pee-pee?"

"No."

At that, Anne opened the car door, took off the child's underwear and told her to pee.

"Outside?"

"Yes, it's okay here."

Even though Anne shielded Naomi from the onlookers, she knew the police officer watched her. The rain pelted down and in the few moments they were out of the car, Naomi was soaked, water dripping from her hair and down her face. Anne wiped her off as best she could.

With Naomi back in her seat, Anne sat behind the wheel and turned the key in the ignition. The police officer loped over to her.

"What are you doing?"

"Turning the heat on. The child is now soaking wet. How much longer?"

"You may go. Apparently everything is in order."

At the first ramp she exited, pulled in at a gas station,

parked and sat, shaking, for long minutes, until her heart slowed and her hands calmed down.

"*Safta*, are we staying here?"

"No, Sweetpea. We're going to a place called Menton."

An hour, she thought. One hour and they would be there. Would Sergio or Esti be waiting? She had nowhere else to go.

* * *

The upright old man, followed by two staff-people and a plainclothes security officer, strode into his office. He gestured the three out of the room. When the phone rang, he recognized the number.

"*Abba*, what have you heard?" Tears choked his daughter's voice. He had nothing to tell her. For two days there had been no word from the agent or the kidnappers.

"Nothing, nothing. They haven't demanded anything new. We believe the Canadian woman is on her own with the child."

"What are you keeping from us?"

"Nothing."

But he was. The mole had betrayed all the safe houses. There was nowhere for the Canadian to run. He hung up and went for a walk to the park near his office. Behind him the building, Knesset, the parliament of free Israel rose like a stockade, surrounded by a high fence meant to keep intruders out, not the Jews in. His friend waited for him, feeding the remains of a sandwich to birds, sparrows perhaps, clustered around the bench.

"So?" he asked when he sat.

"Still running, we think."

"And the mole?"

"We're closing in. One more day."

"The vote is in four days."

"What will you do?" His friend caught his gaze. He slid it away from her to the birds at his feet.

"We shall see. My daughter called me again. I may abstain."

"Will that save her life?" His old friend reached across and took one gnarled fist in her hand.

"Perhaps not."

"The child's life against peace. Is that the choice?"

"I suspect she is dead." His voice trailed off on his last words.

"We may hear otherwise before the vote." She gave his hand another shake and stood up and walked away.

What did she mean? 'We may hear otherwise.' Did she know something he didn't? Whom could he trust?

* * *

The next time Esti woke, the bed had stopped moving, a warm blanket was tucked around her and an intravenous ran cold in her left arm.

"You're with us again, Esti." A woman in white, a stethoscope at the ready, loomed over her.

"Yes." The word came out as a squawk. Her tongue stuck to the roof of her mouth. "Water, please."

The nurse held a straw to her lips and she sucked in half a glass of tepid water before the nurse took it away.

"How long was I out?"

"About two hours. When they brought you in they said you'd been in and out all the way here."

"What city?"

"Nimes."

160

Nimes. It had been ahead of her. She had to get back to her car and her weapons before the guy in the garage decided to open her case.

She wore a hospital gown.

"Where are my clothes?"

"In a bag under the stretcher. We'll take them with us when we go to your room."

"I don't want to stay." She struggled to sit up but fell back on the pillow.

"We can't possibly let you go. You have a concussion."

"Fractures?"

"No, but—"

"I want to get dressed."

"I'll get the doctor."

Good, Esti thought. The doctor wouldn't hurry and she could dress.

She sat up and swung her legs over the side. Another wave of dizziness pulsed over her and she hung on until it passed. She reached for her clothes and dragged out her jeans and then her tee-shirt and jacket. Her phone. Where was her phone? She searched past her shoes and found it in the bottom of the bag. She heard voices outside her cubicle and waited, but they moved on.

She parted the curtains and saw an exit sign at the other end of the room, past three more stretchers. She groped her way to the door. When she stumbled through, she was in a hallway crowded with empty stretchers and poles. All the voices were behind her. She drew a breath, fought down the nausea that was coming in waves again, and made her way to the door. No guards.

A row of three taxis idled at the curb.

She opened the back door of the nearest and fell inside.

"Can you take me to this service station?" She passed him the card.

"Cost you. That's a fifty kilometers."

"Yes." She had a hundred euros under the insoles of her shoes. She slipped one off and retrieved the bill.

"Off we go," he said after tucking the money into his jean pocket.

Esti opened her phone. Still charged. She dialled Colette.

"Yes."

"A problem. A traffic accident on the A-9."

"Are you injured?"

"A mild concussion. I'm going to recover the vehicle and my belongings."

"They will not be pleased."

"Fuck them." She pounded the phone on the seat back. The driver, alarmed, glanced at her.

"It was an accident, Colette. Not my fault."

"Time is running out. The vote is in four days."

"I know. I'll get it done."

"Sergio?"

"Waiting for me." At least she hoped he was.

"Call when you near Menton."

Esti hit the button for Sergio.

"Yes, Esti."

"I have sent you the address. Wait for me."

She settled back in her seat and slept, waking with a jerk when the cab driver called her.

"We're here, lady."

Esti struggled out and into the office.

An hour later she drove into the courtyard of a hotel and checked in. A headache blurred her vision and ruined her concentration. If she didn't rest, she'd have another accident. Sergio would wait and a few hours or a night made no difference. By noon tomorrow, the woman and child would be dead.

CHAPTER 24

The French Riviera formed a lazy crescent from Nice to Menton, a town close to the Italian border. At the turn of the 19th Century, tuberculosis victims sought its lovely climate in hope of defeating their devastating illness. In WWI the palaces and villas sheltered soldiers recovering from war wounds. Menton's storied past included liberation from the Nazis by the Devil's Brigade, a US—Canadian Special Forces unit.

Tall, pastel-colored buildings with red tile roofs, punctuated by a baroque church tower, clustered between the sea and the mountains. The address of the safe house took Anne north of the city to a grey-shuttered, salmon-pink villa. Rain poured from the roof and art-deco balcony. From the driveway, around the corner of the building, she glimpsed the Mediterranean, its angry grey swells pounding the beach in front of the town. She lifted Naomi who was sleeping in her car seat, the donkey clutched under her chin, and rushed in.

Quite luxurious for a safe house, she thought, given her limited experience—balconies and a view of the sea. She searched for a light switch on the wall in the dark interior.

A lamp across the room switched on. Who? A cold shiver ran through her. She clutched Naomi and turned her away from the man in the chair. All the running and there sat Sergio, his gun pointed at her.

"Put her down," he whispered.

Anne lay Naomi on the sofa, covered her with a blue wool throw and tucked her donkey in beside her. She turned to face Sergio, expecting a bullet at any moment.

"What now?" she said. She strained to get the words out, past the lump forming in her throat, to hide her fear. Her dry tongue stuck to her teeth, her lungs ached. She'd forgotten to breath.

"Esti is coming to kill you."

Esti was coming. What did he mean? What about him? Wasn't he going to kill her?

"I need your help," he said.

"My help? How can I help you? Why should I help you?" She paced a little away from Naomi.

"Because I won't kill the child, and she will. Sit down."

"Why? Why will she kill her?" She chose a chair near the balcony, across the room from where the child lay.

"She thinks I'm going to sell her." He darted a glance at Naomi but kept the gun pointed at Anne.

No. Not that.

"And are you?"

"No. I'm going to take her home with me, to my mother."

He whispered still. He must not want Naomi to hear him and start crying, if she understood at all.

"Why?"

"I want to quit this and go home. I want her to think I'm a good man who has a child, a granddaughter for her." His face twisted, in pain she supposed, and he gasped his words.

"A good man who has killed me."

"Or not, if you help me before she comes."

Sweat beaded on his forehead and glistened on his pale cheeks. The hand holding the gun shook as a tremor ran over his body. He was infected, Anne thought. What with? Was Naomi at risk from that too?

"What's wrong with you?"

"The Israeli shot me before he died. In my left arm. I want you to take it out."

"I'm not a surgeon."

"Then you'll die not being a surgeon."

Supplies, she thought.

"I'll need medical supplies."

"In the kitchen."

The emergency kit lay open on the granite counter. Everything in this place was high-end. Once she had a scalpel in her hand, maybe... No, he would shoot her and take Naomi.

She heated water in a kettle on the range. The scalpel, the gloves, and the rest of the equipment were all disposable, except for the blood he would surely lose. A blue plastic container held antibiotics, strong ones, and analgesia—something like Tylenol #3's, she thought. Alcohol in a 500cc bottle.

"Show me," she said.

He rolled up his sleeve. A rough bandage, soaked with pus, overlay the wound. She pulled on a pair of plastic gloves and dropped the putrid dressing into a plastic bag at her feet.

Staphylococcus, she thought. His arm was swollen above and below the entry wound.

"This will hurt," she said. "A lot. Bite on this when you have to." She placed a roll of bandage between his teeth, ignoring the gun, inches away from her face, his finger on the trigger. "I don't want you to shoot me when the pain gets bad. Can't you take your finger off the trigger? I don't have a gun."

He released his grip on the trigger. He grunted but didn't move when she poured alcohol on the wound, and cleaned it with sterile cotton from the medical pack. Pus oozed from the puckered entry wound, the surrounding tissue swollen and red with streaks extending upwards towards his shoulder. She probed the muscles around the wound, searching for the bullet.

"Why didn't it go through?" she asked.

He spat out the cotton roll. "A ricochet, I think. Don't put that back in my mouth."

"I'm going to dig for the bullet now. Be ready for the pain."

She pushed on both sides of the wound, used fine scissors as a probe inside the opening. She felt the slug before she saw it inching upwards towards her. Sergio grunted again and whispered in Spanish. Prayers, she thought.

The tweezers she used next slipped off the bullet. She pushed harder and then she had the ugly lump of metal, stinking of infection.

"It's out, Sergio."

She washed the pus and blood from his arm, dressed the wound, gave him a shot of antibiotic and wiped his face.

"Thank you," he said. He collapsed against the soft cushion of the chair. "Thank you."

"Now what?" But he didn't answer.

"Sergio?"

He was so young. His dark lashes splayed across a face grey with pain. She covered him with a blanket and sat beside him, her hand on his pulse until Naomi woke up and called her. Later when Thomas would ask her why she hadn't left, she could only say that he was her patient and she couldn't. But mostly, it was because he was so young and and wanted to take Naomi to his mother and wanted to be a good man. But what would he want when the pain was gone?

She relaxed against the couch but when she raised her leg, she stifled a scream. The swelling on her shin spread upwards towards her knee, violet-red and tender. Strep, she thought. In her years of working she'd cared for three patients with flesh-eating disease. One lost an arm.

She took two antibiotic tablets, gave herself a shot of another, washed her leg with antiseptic, wincing as the liquid hit the open wound, smoothed on antibiotic ointment and wrapped her calf with bandage. That would have to do. She stashed the rest of the syringes, vials of injectable antibiotic, and ointment in her backpack.

Sergio's gun lay on the carpet. She carried it to the terrace, removed the magazine, and walked to the terrace. She hurled both as far as she could and waited for morning, gazing out over the black expanse of the sea.

CHAPTER 25

Day Thirteen

Thomas walked to the *Place de la Republique*. He'd waited in Perpignan for two days. Any longer and he'd be a local. Masses of yellow and deep pink flowers hung from the base of the statue—an idealized woman symbolizing the Republic—over the water of the fountain arcing into the basin below. He sat in a blue plastic chair at a cafe and drank an espresso, watching the early morning life of the town: children on their way to school, kicking a soccer ball; waiters opening umbrellas; a few women, baskets on their arms, strolling between the patisserie and the butcher's. He paid the waiter and returned to his car. He'd lingered long enough. But where would he go? East, he supposed. Anne would still be going east.

He phone buzzed.

"Tom, the next is Limoux. My source says the list is compromised and they told Ari. He'll be moving. After this, they'll wait for him to contact them. By the way, they call him Daniel. Whether that's a change of identity or his real name, I don't know."

"Thanks."

"Hurry, Tom. I don't think you have much time."

He drove across the brown water of the Aude River on the centuries-old bridge and through the eastern half of the town, following the GPS. A few kilometers further, he turned left onto a minor road. Police tape blocked the lane that led to the stone cottage at the address Quin had given to him, and a crowd of five or six onlookers peered at the policeman guarding the house. He joined them. A gray-haired woman, wearing a flowered dress and a white apron, narrowed her black eyes at him.

Sharp, he thought. She'd know him again. What else did she see?

"What happened here?" he asked her.

"A shooting two days ago. A man is dead, or dying."

"Who lived there?"

The police officer shouted at the crowd to move along. Assorted grumblings broke out, mostly about it being a free road, and what harm was it, but the people returned to their cars and left.

"No one. It was empty for a long time but a big car, a black Mercedes, drove in two days ago, and then a motorcycle."

"Did they both leave before the shooting or did the police get them?"

The officer bellowed again and strode down the lane.

She shook her head and turned towards the farmhouse and said, "The Mercedes left but the man walked back."

She checked the traffic and marched across the highway. Thomas kept pace with her. Ahead, down a narrow lane, stood a stone farmhouse, no larger, he thought than two rooms and a bath.

"Can you describe him?"

She halted.

"Why are you asking so many questions?" she asked.

"Press."

Her eyes widened and she pursed her lips.

"Then my story has some value to you?"

"Yes." Thomas passed her a twenty euro note and waited.

"Tall, blonde, careful."

"Careful?"

"Yes, watching."

"Where is your hospital?"

"For this, Carcassonne. The Good God will care for him but I must go. My man wants his dinner." She tucked the money into her apron pocket and marched away towards her tiny home.

He needed to talk to Daniel, if he still lived. Anne fled on her own, if the cartel didn't take her and the child. He sat behind the wheel, sobbed once, and drove.

* * *

Thomas took a four lane highway, the D-118 to Carcassonne, merged with the *Autoroute des Deux Mers*, and followed a hospital sign that pointed around a golf course to the Center Hospitalier Antoine Gayraud. The grey walls and slate-black turrets surrounding the old city, a world heritage site, loomed ahead of him. He parked and half-walked, half-ran three hundred meters to the entrance. Weatherbeaten signs advertised a new hospital currently being built.

They needed one here, he thought, entering a lobby that segregated staff behind high windows. Linoleum, worn through to the black undercoat, covered the floor. A woman sat on a wooden bench, a red, chapped hand stroking the dark curls of the child on her lap. Other patients and families, their faces stoic and hopeful, crowded the space.

He spoke through a grate to a nurse peering at a computer screen.

"I think the tourist renting the place next to mine was brought in the day before yesterday, shot. I'm worried about his wife and child. Do you know if they accompanied him?"

"What is the man's name?"

"Daniel. Maybe Goldberg?"

She scrolled down a page on her screen and asked him to wait. When she disappeared into the Emergency area, he hurried along the hall, slipped through the door and followed her. She spoke to a police officer standing in front of one of the cubicles. Christ, still in the ER after surgery, he thought.

When the officer walked back to the reception desk with the woman, Thomas ducked behind the curtain. Daniel lay unmoving on a stretcher, his body's vitality recorded in the monitors that counted out his pulse and breathing in muted notes. He opened his eyes when Thomas spoke his name.

"Tom?"

"Yes. Where are they?"

"Menton. Rue de la Republique, #2507. Go."

Thomas slipped into the next cubicle. A couple standing beside a child watched, open-mouthed but silent, as he parted the curtain and left. In the corridor he sprinted for the exit, making it through before the cop returned.

He swung into the driver's seat of a car idling under

a no parking sign, U-turned and drove to the entrance to the parking lot, abandoned the vehicle and ran to his.

By the time a lone police constable reached the stolen vehicle, he was paying the ticket and leaving.

At the Autoroute, he took the on-ramp south to the coast.

Pain shot through his fingers and he loosened his white-knuckled grip on the steering wheel. He willed his breathing to slow. He was getting too old for this. No more. No more.

* * *

Two hours after leaving Carcassonne, Thomas stopped at a service center outside Nimes for gas and carried an espresso to a table in the shade. He was going to need some backup. If something happened to him, who would help her get the child back to Israel and her back home? Not Quin. Too many favors all ready and he'd need permission. Not too likely. Winston? He had no reason to think that Winston would be able to handle an armed encounter or if, as he suspected, he were a cop of some kind, he might not agree to let him deal with it. The police? Same thing and what if the commander in Setenil issued a false warrant for her.

So Adam. He called Vermont.

"Adam? Tom Beauchamp. Do you remember the backup I thought I might need? It's time. She has herself in a helluva mess. Can you get here?"

"Where?"

"I think Marseille, and then rent a car. I'll tell you later where to meet. Don't worry about the cost; get on the next plane out."

"Call me tomorrow. I'll be in France."

Thomas disconnected. He'd done all he could. He got back on the four-lane. Three hours to Menton.

* * *

Adam slipped his phone back in its case. Across the breakfast table—this week a scrubbed pine table from Quebec—Erin raised her eyebrows at him.

"Tom Beauchamp," he said. "He needs my help and wants me to fly to France."

"What help can you be to him in France?" Her eyebrows knitted in frown and her eyes widened. Her oval face, always pale, drained of color.

"Anne's in trouble and he wants to help her, but he can't do it on his own."

"The police?"

"I'm not sure what's going on, but I think the Israeli, Ari, is involved. A kidnapped child's at the center of all this."

"Oh, no. So you're going." She reached across the table and he took her hand.

"Yes. I'll get on a plane today to New York and out this evening to Paris and on to Marseille tomorrow."

"Marseille. Isn't that a city riddled with drugs and violence?"

"It used to be. I don't know about now. Don't worry, love."

After a few moments he freed his hand and called an airline.

By afternoon he was on a flight to New York.

At 8 p.m. he leaned back in a business class seat on Air France, wondering how he was going to back Thomas up without a weapon.

Chapter 26

Sometime in the night, Naomi whimpered. Anne went to her and then dozed in an armchair with Naomi snuggled into her lap. She stirred as a phone rang and she woke to a dawn that touched the Mediterranean with amber and flooded the cloudless sky with clear orange. She carried Naomi to the sofa and settled her again. She brushed damp curls away from the child's forehead. Sergio woke when the phone rang again, reached for it and pushed the answer button.

"*Si.*"

A moment of listening and he said, "I'm waiting outside the villa. How long will you be?"

He grinned. "Yes, I'll wait. What do you want me to do if she leaves?"

He ended the call.

Anne touched his wrist, searching for his pulse. It pounded under her fingers, strong and steady. The fever had broken in the night, leaving his forehead cool.

"Do you feel better?" she asked.

"Yes. But now we have to plan. She is coming."

"Are you still going to kill me?"

"No. After you helped me and stayed with me? No. Go."

"I can't, Sergio. I can't leave her any more than I could leave you. If you truly want to be a good man, let us both go. Go back your mother and find a woman and make babies. Naomi is old enough to tell people who she is. She remembers more and more every day."

He sat up and stared at his fingers.

"Where's my gun?"

"I threw it from the terrace. You passed out for a while."

"Why didn't you leave."

"You're my patient. I couldn't leave you."

He struggled to his feet.

"I can't go back."

"Why not." Anne twisted to keep him in sight.

"They'll find me; Esti will find me and kill me." He sobbed, and hid his face from her.

"Do they know who you are? Where you came from?"

"Maybe." He sat opposite her, his forehead gripped by his good hand.

"You can't stay here." She touched his knee.

"Where are you going?"

"I can't tell you." She stood then, watching the dawn spread over sea. The azure of the Mediterranean returned as the brilliant glow receded. The morning air carried salt and lemon. So peaceful.

"Go. Take the child," Sergio said.

"What will you tell Esti? What did she say to do if we tried to leave?" She turned back to him.

"Kill you both." His dark eyes sought hers. "Go."

Her fear rushed back and she ran to gather Naomi and the donkey into her arms and race out the door. She didn't look back. Half-running, half-walking on the crushed stone of the driveway, Anne carried Naomi to the car. How warm she was. From sleep, or something worse? When she strapped her in the car seat, Anne touched her head and her hands. A fever. What now?

"Naomi, are you feeling sick."

"My tummy hurts."

"Like you fell down or like you're going to throw up?"

"Throw up?"

"When the food comes back up out of your tummy when you're sick?"

"Yes. And I have to go poo."

Anne lifted her out of her seat and ran back into the villa.

"What are you doing?"

"She's sick."

She held Naomi while she vomited. Afterwards, she laid her on the couch and probed her abdomen. Not appendix. In the emergency supplies she found diphenhydramine. Perhaps that would be enough.

"Now go," Sergio said. "Esti is coming. She texted that she's thirty minutes away."

Anne hurried with Naomi to the car, strapped her in and placed a bowl beside her.

"If you're going to be sick again, tell me and I'll stop. Try to use the bowl."

"I want to go home. I want my ima." For the first time since they'd left the donkey pasture, Naomi was crying.

Too few tears, Anne thought. She'd have to stop at a pharmacy and get some rehydration packets and some water.

"We're going, Sweetpea. We're going."

Naomi's sobs faded to a quiet whine and then silence. She was sleeping, her long wet lashes stuck to her cheeks and she had her thumb in her mouth.

Where should she go?

She drove into the center of Menton, along streets bordered with tall narrow houses, in the salmon and dust reds and greens of the Mediterranean. On Rue de la Republique, she found the green cross sign for a pharmacy, parked and carried Naomi with her into the old-fashioned shop. At the desk she asked to speak to the pharmacist.

"My granddaughter is ill," she said. "Perhaps a rotovirus? I need rehydration packets and water for her."

"Certainly, Madame. Has she voided today?"

Anne knew that pharmacists in France were highly trained in medicine and could deal with many issues without involving a doctor.

"Yes, and she cried. She vomited until there was nothing except yellow bile and she had a large diarrheal stool, so she needs rehydration."

"How long has this been, more than a day?"

"No, only been a few hours, but we're driving and I need a room until she's well enough to travel."

"I noticed that you are limping and you seem to be in pain. Can I help?"

"Thank you, but I have antibiotic for it—just a gash."

"A friend runs a bed and breakfast around the corner. Shall I call for you?"

"That would be so kind."

A few minutes later, the keeper of the inn showed her to a tall, narrow room overlooking the sea. The shutters stood open and mild sea air wafted through. The woman brought Anne a bowl and towels.

"Thank you," Anne said. "I didn't know what I was going to do."

Naomi lay on the bed, a white sheet tucked around her, her drying curls lying over her pale forehead. Anne mixed the rehydration formula and sat beside her.

"Naomi, you must take a little of this," she said.

Naomi turned her head away.

"I don't want to be sick any more."

"This will make you better. Try just a little."

What would she do, if she didn't recover? Would there be alerts at hospitals? Would they believe her documents? She caught her breath before it escaped as a sob. Naomi's dark-circled, dull eyes gazed up at her but she took a few sips. In the morning they would go to the hospital and all would be over for her, but Naomi would be safe.

* * *

Esti stopped her car a hundred meters from the villa. Palm trees lined the narrow road and scarlet flowers filled the pots in front of the houses. Most stood shuttered behind gates and hedges. Nothing moved. Too early, she supposed. Where was Sergio? He was supposed to be outside.

The door to the villa stood ajar. Had he all ready killed them and left the mess for her to clean up? She shoved open the door, smashing it on the wall behind, the crash echoing through the house. She crept further in, expecting a word, a scream, a cry from the child.

French doors opened to the terrace overlooking the sea where a figure sat, silhouetted by the bright morning light.

"Come in, Esti." Her heart jumped into her throat and she froze in mid-stride, crouched and pointed her gun at the chair ahead.

"Sergio?"

"Yes."

She relaxed and moved past him. His face, drawn and pale against the yellow seat-back, turned towards her.

"What happened to you?"

"Shot. Infected. I'm better now."

Better. This was better?

"She shot you? The woman?"

"No, the Israeli agent. I forced her take out the bullet."

Esti leaned back the balcony. Her gun, heavy with its silencer, dragged at her right arm. She unscrewed the silencer and tucked it in her pocket and the gun in her jeans.

"Where are the bodies?"

"I passed out and she left in the night."

"Left. For where? What were you thinking? Why didn't you shoot her when she was done?"

What would the bosses in Switzerland or wherever they were, do now? And what about their lives, hers and Sergio? Would someone come after them? She sank to the floor of the terrace. The stone of the balustrade behind her leaked cold into her body.

"Rome, I think. She wants to return the child to Israel and she's afraid of the French police, so she'll go to the closest embassy."

"Not Milan?"

"No."

"Marseille?"

"Too afraid to go back."

"How bad are you?" Maybe she should shoot him. No. That would need even more explanation and she would leave something, hair or cells or something, behind and she didn't have time to clean up.

"I'll be all right. Antibiotics. I think she shot me with sedative when she took out the bullet."

He didn't look all right. He looked like death was coming, but that was not her concern. Hers was to find the woman. Damn. Colette, again.

"What are you going to do?" she said.

"Disappear."

"Where?"

"Can't disappear if someone knows where you're going."

"I must tell them."

"Tell them I'm dead." His eyes, older than when she last saw him, pleaded with her. He moved his arm towards her, but he jerked it back before he touched her. His face twisted and sweat beaded on his forehead.

"I can arrange that."

"Too much mess."

"I'm going. Perhaps Colette has an address in Italy."

She uncoiled herself and left, striding across the blue-tiled floor to the door, out and down the street to her car. On her way to the Autoroute, she called Colette.

"The woman and child escaped. Sergio is dead. He said Rome before he died."

"Did you kill him?"

"No, I found him dying." She'd lied to them.

"Wait. We are sending another team."

"Why?"

"Sergio's body, and the woman."

"No. I pushed him into the sea." Could Colette hear the lie?

"Wait."

Esti drove on, towards the Italian border, just a short stroll away. People walked from Menton into Italy to restaurants. She chose a route that would take her south to Rome.

* * *

Thomas passed the wreckage of a car near Puget sur Argens. A vehicle-removal crew had loaded it onto a flatbed and one man collected orange pylons and stacked them along the shoulder of the road. Anne. Could it be Anne's car? He pulled ahead and stopped. He was met by a torrent of French, the men telling him to return to his vehicle.

"What kind of car? My wife and child..." His voice faltered and his eyes sought the blackened metal of the wreck on the flatbed. The foul scent from the vehicle hit him, bringing with it a wave of nausea.

"A Ford. A man, not a woman inside. No child. It is not your family, Monsieur. Please return to your car."

Thomas ran back to his car and sat for a moment to quiet his pounding heart and fight off the threatened vomit. The horn of the truck sounded behind him, he put the car in gear and drove. He'd be in Menton in an hour or so. The sun, rising ahead of him, turned the sky the color of blood oranges he ate in Morocco.

Far below, Menton stretched along the sea in tiered ranks of red tile roofs and sulphur yellow and tangerine walls that rose from the ruined castle by the harbor. Ahead of him lay the tunnel. He took an off-ramp to the north end of the city and the address of the safe house.

A woman with short blond hair and giant sunglasses tore past him in a red Mercedes SL. Esti had long black hair, he thought, but on this road... He left the car a few meters from the address, strode up, and pushed the door open. He scanned the room.

A man sat on the terrace, his back towards Thomas. Thomas crept across the tiles and held a gun to the man's head.

"Where is she?" Thomas moved around in front, and asked again. "Where is she?"

"Who?"

"The woman with the child."

"Anne. She helped me; she fixed my arm."

"Where is she?" Thomas whispered, his throat tight and his breathing on hold waiting for the answer.

"Gone. She wouldn't tell me where."

"You just let her go?"

"She helped me and she could have escaped but she stayed so I wouldn't die. Yes, I let her go." He was yelling now, sweating and wild-eyed.

"Take it easy, Sergio. You're Sergio, aren't you?"

Sergio sat back, wiped his face on his sleeve and nodded.

"Where did she go?"

"'I don't know. Esti was here. I told her Rome."

"That wasn't true?"

"She will kill them both. She thought I wanted to sell the child. I wanted to keep her, take her to my mother, to save her." He sobbed, heaving cries muffled by an arm thrown across his face.

"Where did Anne go."

"She didn't tell me."

"How far ahead?"

"An hour, no more."

Thomas left him, returned to his car and called Quin.

"Quin? Tom. Not at Menton. Any further safe house?"

"Not that I've heard. I'll call again."

Thomas drove out of Menton and into Italy, stopping across the border at a cafe in a service center. Where would she go now? Why wouldn't she call *Mossad* for help?

* * *

When Thomas left, Sergio took his bike from the hiding place he found when he arrived. He sat, helmeted and watchful as a black Mercedes SUV drove along the street near the villa. Two men crept up on the house, one circling towards the sea, the other to the front door he left open. He heard a shout, and the second man pounded around and in. Moments later, they walked back, one of them with his phone to his ear.

Their bird has flown, Sergio thought and waited until they pulled away. Five minutes later, he drove past the house where he regained his freedom to the road that would take him back to Spain. At a bridge, he stopped and tossed into the river below all his identification as Sergio and from a hidden compartment on the bike restored the documents identifying him as Carlos Valdez, a citizen of Madrid.

He would stay at his mother's house for a few days, and go on into Madrid and find a job, any job. He saved the money they'd paid him in a bank account in Switzerland. Plenty to start a new life, maybe a shop.

On a steep mountain-side, halfway through the Pyrenees, the black SUV came up beside him and swerved. The bike flew off the mountainside. Sergio's last thought was to regret he hadn't sent his mother the account number. Then he hit the rocks.

CHAPTER 27

Day Fourteen

Twelve hours later, after a night of cajoling Naomi to take spoonsful and then sips and finally an entire glass of rehydration liquid, Anne drifted off to sleep for a few moments. A dream, of Bermuda and firing the gun in the dark woke her. She checked Naomi. Her fever was down and then Anne slept too.

"*Safta*, wake up. It's morning."

Naomi stood beside her, patting her shoulder. Anne took the hand in hers. Cool. Naomi's eyes were bright.

"I'm hungry."

"I'm sure you are. We'll eat after your bath."

"Where are we going, *Safta*? Are we going to get Daniel? Why did Sergio tell us to go? Why did we stop here?" Naomi piped her questions as Anne buckled her into her seat.

"You were sick, Naomi, but now we're going to Italy. That's another country just over there." Anne pointed east.

"Will Abba be there?"

"No. Some people will bring him to us when I call them, but first we have to drive a little way."

"Will Daniel come?"

"No, Daniel is still sick." Anne settled herself in the driver's seat. Naomi's big-eyed frightened face looked at her from the mirror. She adjusted the image away and drove.

"Will Sergio chase us?"

"No, he's going home to his mommy, too."

Ahead of them on the A-8 loomed the last tunnel before the Italian border. The long tunnel, brightly lit along its rounded length, was one-way so she didn't have to deal with oncoming traffic. The mass of rock above them weighed down on her. But traversing took only a couple of minutes and they burst into the sunshine of an Italian morning on the Pont Saint Louis. The tollbooths for the *Autostrada dei Fiori*, the A-10, lay ahead. She bought a ticket and drove east.

Safe. They were safe from the police for now. No one knew they had entered Italy, except Sergio, and he was leaving to save himself. An hour of the rushing morning traffic and a sequence of tunnels later, the cars ahead of her slowed. It was time to get off the four-lane and find the farm. She paid at the tollbooth, took the off ramp and at its crest saw what had held up the traffic: a police roadblock. For her? Who would know unless Sergio...?

The route she wanted to follow led up into the hills north of the A-10 but to the south lay the town Pietra Ligure and Naomi needed food and some time out of the car and perhaps a run on the beach.

"I'm hungry," said the sleepy voice from the back seat. "Are we there?"

"Not yet. We're going to eat and walk on the beach."

Pietra Ligure, another smallish town of red tile roofs and pastel walls, nestled between hills and the green waters of the sea. On the crescent of the beach, lounge chairs were drawn up in rows between furled umbrellas. A chaotic mix of couples, dogs, children and vendors strolled along the sand.

Anne and Naomi ate at a cafe by the sea and afterwards walked for an hour, Naomi teasing the waves and giggling as each one chased her back. They came upon a shack selling children's beach clothes and accessories. Naomi chose a pink and purple sequined backpack and they filled it with shorts and tee-shirts and a warm fleecy jacket and another long cover-up in green terry cloth.

"Can I keep these when I go home, *Safta?*" she asked, turning her face up and smiling, her eyes hidden behind enormous sunglasses.

"Of course. They belong to you."

Naomi skipped happily beside her on the way back to the car, singing to her donkey. Anne limped beside her. Still painful. If the oral antibiotics didn't cure it she might lose her leg. She shook off the fear and set her GPS for Tovo San Giacomo, a village in the hills. There, Daniel said, she would find the old woman and safety.

* * *

Adam flew on a commuter jet to Marseille, arriving in bright sunlight. After he checked in at a hotel, he sat at a cafe on the beach, watching the crowds and enjoying an espresso. Palm trees waved in an onshore breeze, and the babble of voices mixed French with languages he recognized, like German and Russian and those he didn't, from Africa and Asia.

He dialled Thomas's number.

"Tom? Adam."

"Where are you?"

"Marseilles."

"Rent a vehicle and drive over here, to Menton."

"Where's Menton?"

"Just to the east of you. At the border."

"How long?"

"Less than thirty minutes."

"What hotel are you at?"

Thomas shook Adam's hand, walked out on the terrace and stared over the sea.

"What's up?"

"She's in the wind. She ran from Menton and no one seems to know the next safe house."

"So what do we do?"

"Wait. I have a couple of sources working on it. The guy who came for her was wounded. She fixed his arm with a gun on her, but stayed to care for him. He couldn't believe it and he let her go."

"That's Anne. So?"

"She's going to Italy. We'll cross the border to Pietra Ligure and wait."

CHAPTER 28

Anne followed *Strada Provinciale 4*, a narrow highway in the hills to Tovo San Giacomo. Her route switchbacked through the village that stretched along the road. Beyond the houses, olive trees dotted the fields.

Past the village, ancient stone walls stopped the timeworn hills from tumbling onto the road and low barriers of steel separated the car from the valley below. When her breathing quickened and her heart started to race, she concentrated on the late flowering shrubs blooming pink and scarlet on the shoulders of the highway. Somehow she had to get over this paralyzing terror of heights. There was no room in her life now for vague fears.

She passed another village, Mogliolo, and resumed the dizzying drive through the hills. She thought Naomi was sleeping but in the rearview saw that she watched the fields go by, rubbing the ears of her donkey.

On a hill no more than a kilometer from her destination, the engine gave a sad wheeze, and lost power. Just ahead the shoulder widened. She wedged the car into it, between two outcroppings of rock.

"Naomi, we're walking the rest of the way."

"No more car seat?"

"No more car seat."

The child's face broke into a delighted smile. How she must have hated being cooped up in the seat, but she hadn't whined once.

Naomi clambered out after Anne changed her sandals for running shoes. Anne took the pistol and its cartridges out of the glove box and pushed them down into the pocket of her jacket. She strapped on their backpacks and walked. Halfway up the hill they passed a white building with heavy wires leading to and from it. Perhaps a switching station, Anne thought, feeding power along the remote valleys.

Far below, an ancient farmhouse surrounded by a few rows of olive trees and more of grapevine overlooked the valley and the river. But they still had yet another curve and hill to walk.

"*Safta?*"

"Yes."

"Can you pick me up and carry me?"

"For a little way."

Anne hoisted Naomi onto her left hip and struggled on. Only a kilometer, she thought. She stumbled, pain coursed down her leg and she shifted Naomi's weight. The child's soft hand curl tighter around her neck.

The last hill stood between her and the farmhouse and whatever or whomever waited for her. Fear and pain dragged at her legs and she hesitated.

"Why aren't we going up the hill?"

"We are, in a moment." She twisted Naomi onto her other hip and marched up the hill.

Who would she find at the end? Esti or…Sarah? Daniel said her name was Sarah.

* * *

Thomas parked the car close to the beach at Pietra Ligure,

"So now what?" Adam asked, stretching when he climbed out of his car.

"Wait. On the beach, I think.

They rented chairs and an umbrella and tried to relax. Around them, children built castles and towns and lakes in the sand, some too close to waves that crept up and over their creations. Behind, to the north, rose hills and the Apennine Mountains.

Would Anne go north, Thomas wondered, take the road that wound up into the hills along deep gorges with tors looming over her? Not likely, not unless she were forced too or had somewhere to hide. Would Daniel have told her a place to go off the grid? He might. Perhaps he told Winston.

"I'm going to try a friend of hers in Setenil."

"She made a friend all ready you can trust?"

"I think so."

He called the number Winston gave him, got his service, and left a message.

He tried Quin again, left another message and settled back to wait.

He woke with a start. A child, her red bucket dangling from her hand, stood beside his chair.

"You were asleep," she said.

"Yes. Who are you?"

A mother called and the child scampered back along the sand. How long had he slept? An hour, no more. His phone buzzed and he sat up to answer.

"Tom?"

"Quin, yes. Do you have anything?"

"No. But as soon as she calls *Mossad*, they'll call me."

"Not soon enough. Esti—"

"Yeah. But if they don't know where she is, neither will Esti."

"Maybe."

"I'll call you."

Adam wasn't in the chair beside him but a few moments later walked up with two bottles of beer and two *panini*.

"Quin called. He has nothing."

"Would she go to the Canadian Consulate in Milan?"

"Not likely, with the child and a fake passport."

"Why a fake passport?"

"Daniel, the Israeli would have arranged it."

"You know this how?"

"It's what I would do."

Adam raised an eyebrow but all he said was, "So we wait some more?"

"Yes."

"I'll need a weapon, when it's a go."

"In the bag." He gestured towards the gym bag at his feet.

"Good." Adam opened his beer and unwrapped his *panino*.

Thomas watched the waves crash against the beach. Where the hell was she?

* * *

At the top of the lane that curved down a steep hill to the farmhouse, Anne set Naomi down and straightened her back. Only chickens picking at freshly-thrown feed and a white pickup truck in front of a stone outbuilding suggested someone was home. When they reached the blue front door, she touched a *mezuzah,* an ivory case containing a miniature Torah scroll affixed to the right side of the door frame in a silent prayer of hope for Naomi.

Anne knocked and stood back, holding Naomi's hand. What if Esti answered? Would she be able to defend Naomi against her? She fingered the gun deep within her right-hand pocket and waited. Pull the trigger, he said. The safety is in the trigger. Pull both. The woman who opened the door, the fine parchment of her face as wrinkled as an archaic document, blinked against the light, focussed and said, "Who sent you?"

"Daniel."

"Come in quickly."

Inside, shutters closed against the sun darkened the room. A simple kitchen filled one end, with three faded green cupboards, a deep white sink and a blackened cook stove sitting next to a scrubbed pine table. The other end held a rose-brocaded sofa and a reading lamp behind a wide chair of deep-blue corduroy. Stairs led up from the right.

"Come, sit." The woman locked the door behind her.

Anne sat with Naomi on her knees at the table near the stove and waited. The old woman bustled around, made coffee in a French press and hot chocolate in a battered pot on the stove. She took a tin from the cupboard and offered them *biscotti* studded with almonds.

"How long have you been running?"

"Four days."

"Has the child slept?" She touched Naomi's curls with one long finger, its joints swollen from arthritis.

"Yes, last night in Menton and in the car."

"You are on foot?"

"The car broke down, a kilometer from here. Daniel said to come here because you are not on anyone's list."

"That's true. The child—what is her name?"

"Naomi."

"Put her to rest on the sofa. We must talk."

Naomi finished her cookie, Anne took her to the sofa and covered her with a blanket.

"I'll be right over there," she said, "where you can see me anytime you want to."

The old woman washed the cups before saying, "My name is Sarah."

"Anne, although for the moment I'm Elizabeth."

"Elizabeth. Do you know why Daniel sent you here?"

"The list of safe houses was compromised."

"Yes, but why to me?"

"I don't know."

"Let me tell you."

Sarah's story began in Florence, when she was fifteen. The Italians weren't as anti-Semitic as the people of the north, she said, and her family was safe until 1943. When Italy capitulated and Germany invaded, a roundup of Jews in Florence began.

"My father heard that the Germans were coming and he knew that meant we would all be taken to the camps. By then we knew what they were doing. Before they reached the city, we escaped to Assisi, to my father's brother. A priest, Father Rufino Niccacci, had a plan to save the Jews of the city. He dressed some of us as nuns and taught us Catholic ritual. Others had false papers and lived and worked in the open. At the end of the war, one of the men forged a letter from Marshal

Kettering of the high command declaring Assisi an open city. All the German troops left and Assisi wasn't harmed. Every Jew in the city was saved."

"You lived as a nun for all that time?"

"Yes, and they do not have an easy life, let me tell you. We had other jobs to do. I worked for the resistance as well."

"And after the war?"

"I went to Israel for a few years and joined the fight for a new country, but I was homesick for Italy. We had been integrated into Italian life for many generations and I felt as Italian as I did Jewish. Israel was foreign to me. I returned, to a man who had been in the resistance with me, and married, had two children, but now I am alone here. The children live in Rome."

"And Daniel?"

"Daniel is my brother's grandson. My brother stayed in Israel."

"Thank you for helping us. Naomi is so tired that I hope we can stay for a day or two." Anne looked over at Naomi, who slept with one arm around her donkey.

"You must call *Mossad*."

"They have a mole, a traitor."

"Yes, but the name I will give you is a person who will keep you safe. At least I hope so."

Anne brooded. This was the only way forward, unless she could get the car repaired, and drive on, to the Embassy in Rome, perhaps.

"What about the Embassy?"

"What about it?"

"I could take her there."

"It is a long way to Rome. Rest now, and we'll talk later."

"The car?"

"Also a problem for later. I must show you something."

She took Anne to her bedroom at the back of the cottage. Inside an armoire, she clicked a release and a portion of the back wall moved forward.

"The space here is big enough for a child. If you feel threatened, put her in here."

"She's afraid of the dark."

"There's a light. She seems to me a child who can understand the need to be quiet."

All of these places had a secret hole, a way to evade searchers, a leftover from hiding during the war.

Anne sat beside Naomi on the sofa, Sarah in the armchair. Talk later, Anne thought. Hide the child in the closet. Where was Esti? What was she doing? What resources did the cartel have? Would someone find the abandoned car and trace it back? She dozed off, waking with a start. Thomas. Should she call Thomas?

* * *

Anne awoke to Naomi calling her.

"*Safta? Safta.* Wake up. I want to go pee-pee."

She took Naomi to the bathroom and joined Sarah in the kitchen.

"I think I should call the number now. Will he still be a work?"

"She is called Adina and yes."

Anne walked outside to call.

"Adina. Sarah in Italy gave me your number. The child, Naomi, the kidnapped child, is with me and—"

"I will get someone to talk—"

"No, you—" What was this? Anne leaned against the

196

wall of the house, her eyes on the lane down from the highway. A car slowed and sped away. A watcher?

"I have no authority to bargain—"

"I don't want to bargain; I need help getting her back to you—"

"I'll call—"

"A moment and I'll get Sarah." She marched back into the house.

"Sarah, she's having some trouble with this."

Sarah took the phone and spoke a few words in Hebrew and disconnected.

"They're coming," she said.

"The mole?"

"As yet unknown. They'll be here tomorrow afternoon. I'll take your phone with me to the village in the morning."

"I should call Thomas—"

"No. His phone may be monitored." Anne squeezed her eyes shut and hid them with one hand. She hesitated to call Thomas and now this old woman was telling her she couldn't. Without a phone she would be alone.

"Did Adina tell you?"

"No, that is what must be done. Trust me, Anne."

Sarah sat opposite her. Her gaze caught Anne's and held it.

"Daniel sent me here, not to hide but because you're experienced in this spy business. Didn't he?"

Sarah reached across the table and her fingers, frail and thin, gripped Anne's hand with a hidden strength.

"Trust me. I can help you but you must do what I say."

"I want to call Thomas."

"No, later."

"And if there is no later? He won't know I wanted to call him, to tell him—" What would she tell him? What could she tell him, until she was looking into his eyes?

"No. It's too dangerous. The mole may have learned of your location. We must prepare. Do you have a weapon?"

"Yes, Daniel's, but I've never shot it and I don't know if I can kill another person."

"For Naomi?"

"Perhaps."

"Come outside and I'll show you what to do."

Naomi played with the chickens while Anne and Sarah walked behind the farmhouse. Sarah took the gun from her and showed her how to load it, and passed it over to Anne.

She rubbed her hands over the surface of the gun, cool and smooth under her fingers. It was so simple, putting together this weapon that could rob another person of life. Anne shuddered and gripped harder.

"It won't fire unless you pull the triggers," Sarah said.

"Yes. Daniel told me."

Sarah showed her how to hold the weapon, bracing one hand with the other.

"Look at the center of the person's mass, not at the gun; look at the target. Pull it up and fire at the tree. Now."

Anne jerked her hands up, pulled back on the triggers and fired. She stumbled back from the force of the gun. The acrid smell of the gases enveloped her and the explosion of sound rang in her ears. For a moment she was hiding in the dark in the room in Bermuda, waiting for someone who wanted to kill her, firing the weapon at the sound of his voice. But she hit the tree. A white splinter scarred the silver bark.

"Very good. You must remember what you did. More practice would bring company."

"I will."

A tiny hand plucked at Anne's sleeve.

"*Safta,* why are you shooting?"

"Practice. Don't worry, Naomi. Sarah made some food. Wasn't that nice of her?"

Anne passed the gun back to Sarah and picked up Naomi and carried her back to the house.

Back inside, Naomi crawled up on a chair beside her and Sarah set plates on the table. Anne's stomach tightened and she pushed her plate away.

"You are not hungry?"

"Nerves and I have an infection in my leg."

"Yes. You must trust me we've done enough. Let me see your leg."

"After you eat. It's not a pretty sight."

Anne took up her fork and pulled the plate forward. Trust her? She must. She had no other choice.

"Trust is no longer easy for me, since the episode in Bermuda. I don't feel safe with anyone."

"It will pass. You pushed away the memories of those days, instead of talking about them, working through and making sense of what happened to you and forgiving yourself."

"Forgiving myself?"

"Didn't you have the urge to kill?"

"Or be killed." Why was this old woman telling her she needed to forgive herself. She'd done nothing wrong in Bermuda.

"Yes," said Sarah, and her voice was gentle, "but

you're a person who was about healing, not killing. To deal with that, first you must forgive yourself and trust yourself to do what is right, not according to someone else but according to you, your own beliefs."

"My beliefs tell me guns, shooting and killing are wrong, evil."

"Don't your beliefs also include protecting and saving children?"

"Yes." Did that mean she could and must kill Esti? She'd persuaded Sergio, but Esti was different, more committed. Even Sergio was afraid of her. She ran her hand over Naomi's curls. She would do whatever it took to save Naomi.

Later, Sarah redressed her leg and Anne gave herself an injection of antibiotic. The infection hadn't spread. Her nightmare of streptococcus infection and losing her leg receded. She would survive at least until *Mossad* or Esti arrived.

* * *

They ate a dinner of pasta dressed with basil *pesto*, rosemary and garlic focaccia, and a fish, Ligurian style. Sarah stuffed more rosemary and garlic in the cavity of the fish and laid it on a bed of sliced potatoes in her baking pan. Next, she sprinkled on the remaining ingredients: capers, deep-violet *taggiasche* olives, cherry tomatoes, extra virgin oil and a cup of dry white wine. A glass of the same wine added to the meal. Mediterranean diet, thought Anne, in a two-room farmhouse on the side of a rocky hill. She could eat this forever.

Naomi picked at the pasta, but tucked into the fish.

"Do you eat this food at your home?" Anne asked her.

"My *Ima* cooks it."

"I haven't heard that word for a long time," said Sarah. Her brown eyes, set wide in a face as wrinkled as a fine old leather glove, brimmed with tears, but she wiped them with the tail of her apron, and got up to take the plates away.

"Let me do this," Anne said, carrying her dishes and Naomi's to the sink. Sarah talked to Naomi in Hebrew.

Later, she asked Sarah how much Naomi remembered of her life.

"Most," she said. "As soon as she starts to think in Hebrew again, she remembers. She should be with her family by the day after tomorrow, if the agents get here on time."

"If the agents get here before Esti."

"My friend in Israel will not betray us."

"She has to tell someone."

"I think perhaps Naomi should have a bath and go to bed."

Later, Anne sat in an armchair, watching the last rays of the sun slide behind the hills. Sarah settled in a chair opposite her, resting her feet on a brocade-covered stool.

"What will you do after they take Naomi?" Sarah asked.

"Get the car fixed and drive to the Canadian Consulate in Nice and ask them to help me."

"Perhaps you should call one of the people who helped you escape from Spain. Who were they?"

"Daniel, but he was shot and he may be dead." She shielded her face with her hands and fought to keep away the tears.

"I can find out for you tomorrow morning. Would you like an espresso?" She stood up and walked towards the kitchen.

"Yes, thanks." She'd be up all night, but she wouldn't sleep anyway.

"No one else?"

"A man called Winston Caldwell. British. He helped me in Spain, although he didn't want me involved with the child."

"Why not?"

"He thought there wasn't enough evidence to speak to the authorities and I would get into personal trouble if I did. He's a photojournalist, or says he is, but he behaves more like a cop. And then there's Thomas."

"Thomas?" She handed Anne a tiny yellow cup.

The espresso, laced with something—brandy, perhaps—burned in her throat, but warmed her body.

Sarah took the cups to the kitchen and rinsed them, and placed them on a shelf above the sink.

"Thomas?" she said again.

"Thomas is or maybe was my friend. I got into some trouble in Bermuda."

She told Sarah about Bermuda and Thomas's involvement in the CIA.

"So he didn't tell you?"

"He didn't." Anne turned her eyes away to the view of the dark hills.

"He couldn't. When you're part of that organization, the fewer people outside of it who know who you are, the safer you are and the safer are the people you love. Besides, if you don't mind my saying so, you seem to find trouble by yourself."

"Yes. I would like to call him, but—"

"After tomorrow. Where is he?"

Anne got up and closed the shutters against the darkness and restless, paced the tiny room.

"I thought I saw him arrive at Setenil when Daniel and I were leaving with Naomi, but I was likely mistaken. I wanted to call him, but you took my phone."

"Why do you think you were mistaken? Sit down, Anne. I'm too old to watch you march up and down."

"I'm sorry, Sarah." She sat in the chair close to her and Sarah patted her shoulder.

"You thought you were mistaken?"

"Wishful thinking." Anne closed her eyes and leaned back for a moment. She woke to Sarah calling her.

"Anne, time for bed."

"Oh, gosh. Did I fall asleep while I was talking to you? I'm sorry."

"You lie on the sofa, and I will bring you a pillow and a duvet."

Tomorrow. She would call Thomas tomorrow and he would come.

CHAPTER 29

Day Fifteen

Winston sat in his corner, reading, his back to the stone wall of the terrace. He threw down his newspaper, called the waiter and asked for another espresso. The news article detailed the upcoming vote in Israel about the settlements. In his view, the settlements had gone for enough. The two country solution was needed. The vote was crucial and one man's lead would be followed. And that man had the welfare not only of Israel but also of his granddaughter on his mind. Winston drummed his fingers on the table top, stopping when Juanito returned with his cup.

"You are upset this morning, Senor Caldwell?"

"Yes. I must take a short trip away. I'll be back tomorrow."

He called Henri and caught a private jet from Malaga to Montpellier, rented a car and drove to Carcassonne. He parked in the lot under the weatherbeaten sign promising a new hospital. He paused at the reception window, and asked the way to see Daniel Goldberg.

"I'm sorry. No visitors."

Winston withdrew a wallet from his jacket and showed her his credentials.

"Certainly," she said and gave him instructions.

He rode the elevator, its battered walls testament to years of service, to the third floor. There, he found a guard posted outside the room. He showed his credentials once again. The guard checked with a supervisor before letting him in.

Daniel lay in a standard hospital bed with a view out the window of blue sky and in the distance, hills. An intravenous ran into his left arm. The pallor underlying his tan turned his skin to aged leather.

"Daniel," Winston said.

"You. From Setenil. You're Anne's friend. How did you get in here?" He struggled to sit further up in the bed.

"I showed them this." He passed Daniel the credentials that verified him as an agent of Interpol.

"So?" Daniel raised an eyebrow and reached for a jug on his bedside table. Winston took it and poured some water into a glass and passed it to him.

"So?" Daniel said again.

"Where you have sent Anne? We know the safe houses are blown and you arranged somewhere off the grid. I want to send Thomas to her."

"What happened in Menton?"

"Anne and Naomi escaped."

"Why should I trust you?"

"Use my phone; call Interpol or your own people. I'll wait outside."

"Stay." He took the phone and when connected, said a few words in Hebrew, and waited. Five long minutes later he clicked off.

"Italy." He gave Winston the address of the farm in the hills.

"How are you?" Winston asked.

"I survived. They're taking me home tomorrow."

"When do you think you can get back to work?"

"Never."

Winston offered him his hand and left. At his car, he called Thomas.

"I have a location for you. Is your phone secure?"

"No. I'll call you back."

An hour later, Winston gave Thomas the address in Italy.

* * *

The nurse bustled into the room, steps ahead of two men in dark suits.

"Here are your...colleagues to take you home, Daniel."

Daniel shook hands with the agents, friends from early days. They stayed with him through the transfer by helicopter to an airport outside Montpellier and then to a private jet to Tel Aviv.

By noon, he lay in a secure room in a hospital. One agent stood by his bedside.

"My family?"

"Your brother is bringing Shoshana in a short while. Is the child still alive?"

"When I last saw her, yes."

"The woman? Is she reliable?"

"Yes, reliable and fierce in her protection of the child but without skills. She has a weapon if she reached the car I left for her, but doesn't want to use it."

The long speech exhausted him and he closed his eyes against pain that tunnelled through his belly.

"What else?" he said, without looking at the agent.

"Does she have an ally?"

"I gave her the address for Sarah, in Italy."

"Will she go to her?"

"She'll try."

"Why not the consulate?"

"I didn't know who to trust." Daniel opened his eyes and looked into the face of his old friend.

"I'll have to report where she's going."

"Give her time. If you report and the mole betrays her, Esti will get there before you do."

"Get well, Daniel."

"Protect them."

"I will."

At that the agent left the room. Outside, he dialed his boss's number.

* * *

Esti reached the outskirts of Rome by mid-afternoon. She'd find a place to stay and wait until the people in Switzerland found the woman. If she had the time, that woman's death would not be slow, considering all the trouble she'd been. Her phone signaled a text.

Call the number in Geneva, it read.

First she'd eat. She exited the *Autostrada del Sole* and found a cafe and espresso. After two months in Setenil, with its famous pastries, she rejected the Italian offerings, but chose a *panino* from a glass case.

When she finished her snack, she brushed scattered crumbs from her shirt and clicked on her phone and called.

"Esti?"

"Who else?"

"We have information that she is at this address near the border with France."

"What the hell. All the way back?"

"Yes." The phone disconnected.

Definitely she would take her time with the woman. But night had fallen and she needed sleep before a confrontation with someone she presumed must be an armed agent, not the innocent doctor she pretended to be.

She took the Autostrada North. Past Lucca, the onboard computer warned her of construction on the A-2 ahead of her. She took the exit ramp for Viareggio. The lights of the hotels along the beachfront blazed into the darkness and reminded her she needed sleep. She had a dull headache since she left the hospital, and now her temples throbbed and the traffic lights, each with a halo of gold, dazzled her vision.

She chose a five-story, three-star hotel that fronted on a street away from the Lido, parked and carried her case of weapons with her inside.

"I need a room for a few hours sleep," she said to the clerk. "I've been driving for a long time and I was in a traffic accident."

"We have only one vacancy, but I'm afraid it's our least attractive room."

"As long as it has a bed. I need a wake-up for 5 a.m."

"Not much sleep."

"All I have time for."

The room was just a room: a narrow single bed, a view of the back streets away from the Lido, a bathroom with just room enough for a closet-sized shower. She stood under the shower until it threatened to run cold and then collapsed on the bed. Too soon, the phone beside the bed jangled.

"Five a.m.," said the impersonal voice.

By 6 a.m. she was on the road again. In three hours she would be there.

CHAPTER 30

The next morning, Naomi stood at the side of the sofa, calling her.

"*Safta,* wake up. It's tomorrow."

"Yes, Sweetpea. I'm awake."

Across the room, Sarah took a handbag out the cupboard.

"I'm going for some milk to the farm down in the valley. I won't be long. Lock the door and stay inside."

"Should we come with you?"

"No. Have some coffee and I'll be back in an hour."

"Must you go? It's only milk."

"I must get rid of the cell phone and this is the day I call my daughter. If I don't, she'll worry and send someone."

"Why don't we just disable the phone?"

"I'll put it on a bus. They'll think that you've gone from here."

"Hurry."

"I'll be back in an hour."

Anne checked the clock. It was 9 a.m.

CHAPTER 31

Thomas disconnected from Winston.

"What?" Adam said.

"I have an address. Grab your stuff."

"One car?"

"Yes. I'll meet you downstairs."

He paid the bill at the desk and they were on their way. The dashboard clock read 9:30 a.m.

The road into the hills wound through several hamlets to Tovo San Giacomo. At a roadside cafe, they stopped. He showed the waiter the address Daniel gave him.

"Do you know where this farm is?"

"Yes, it's old Sarah's farm, ahead in the hills. She's going to be busy today. You're the second person to ask for her. She's not home though. I saw her go through on her way to call her daughter a few minutes ago."

"The second person?"

"Yes, a blond woman. Bellissima. Legs up to here." He smacked his lips with a kissing sound and patted the air around his thighs. "And her car. A red Mercedes SL convertible."

"How far ahead of me?"

"Half an hour. If you wait, Sarah will come by. She stops most mornings."

"Thanks, I'll wait for her up there."

He left a few euros on the table and raced out to his car.

"We're half an hour behind the woman, Esti, who's going to kill her."

He revved the car and skidded onto the highway. Half an hour.

* * *

Esti reached Pietra Ligure, and took the off-ramp that led into the old town and down to the beach. The sun warmed the sand and brought out fat pale tourists who were taking morning strolls beside the sea. A cafe's tables reached the sand's edge. She stopped, ordered a glass of water and a pastry and swallowed two more of the pain killers they gave her at the hospital. Her head hurt most of the time now.

At 9:15 a.m. she left five euros on the table and drove up and out of the town.

The GPS took her away from Tovo San Giacomo on a winding road in the hills. At a roadside cafe she asked directions.

A kilometer from her destination, she passed a car drawn up in a lay-by. She stopped and walked back to search. A carseat and maps of Spain and the south of France scattered on the front passenger side suggested she was closing in on the woman. The farmhouse below looked empty. No other vehicles. Perhaps she was alone and an easy target.

Esti rubbed her head and took two more pills. She abandoned her car at the top of the lane and squatted behind a bush, watching the house for long minutes. Nothing outside. No smoke from a stove, but maybe propane had reached this far. She crept down the hill on the blind side, where no windows allowed for watchers. She took her time, careful to avoid the crunch of gravel underfoot. When she reached the house she sidled along the wall and glanced around the back corner. No entrance. She edged towards the front door. A *mezuzah* on the frame explained the flight to this remote area. The woman knew she would find an ally here.

Her breathing quickened and she felt the rush of excitement, of her heart forcing more blood around her body, but her head throbbed and for a moment her vision blurred. Soon she would be inside. She depressed the lever of the door-handle. Locked. The element of surprise would be gone if she forced her way in, but did she need that? The farmhouse was simple, only one entrance. No escape for the woman, no hiding the child from her. She stood back and fired at the lock.

* * *

Inside the farmhouse, Anne washed dishes from breakfast. She'd take Naomi for a walk when Sarah came back, if there was anywhere to go. She took some scraps out to a compost heap beside an outbuilding across the farmyard. A movement caught her eye, high on the hill near where she had abandoned her vehicle.

A red car crept along the highway. Searching. A woman at the wheel. Was it Esti? She stopped at the end of the lane. It must be her. Anne tossed the scraps and ran back to the farmhouse. She locked the door behind her and closed and barred the shutters. How long until Esti would be here? Minutes. Less.

"Naomi, come. You must hide. Esti is here."

"Why do I have to hide from Esti?"

"She wants to take you back to Setenil. She won't let me take you home." She hustled Naomi into the back room and into the space behind the wall of the armoire. She clicked on the light.

"Be very quiet, Naomi. Don't call for me or she will hear you. If she calls for you, don't answer. Sarah will come back soon."

Big-eyed, Naomi nodded. Tears floated on her eyes but she didn't cry, didn't ask to stay with Anne. What else had she been through, Anne wondered.

She closed the wall and then the armoire door. She leaned her head against it for a moment before she ran back to the kitchen. She took Daniel's gun out of the pocket of her jacket and waited.

* * *

Thomas's car roared up the switchbacks and stopped beside the abandoned vehicle. Inside: a carseat, maps, a pink blanket.

"Tom, this could be anyone's car," Adam said when he joined him.

"The house is down there, where the red Mercedes is blocking the lane."

"Is that Esti?" Adam asked, pointing to a blond woman who climbed out of the car and stood for a moment.

She crept down the lane, glanced around the back of the house and moved towards the front door. No smoke escaped from the chimney; shutters blocked the windows; chickens scratched in their pen: perhaps no one was home. Perhaps Esti would think so too and leave without entering. He couldn't wait to find out.

"I don't know."

He drove the kilometer on but cut the engine at the top of the lane to the farmhouse and rolled down as far as Esti's car, blocking it from the road. "Stay here. Watch the back and get her if she comes out."

"Alive?"

"Not necessary."

He was running towards the farmhouse when he heard a shot, and then another.

* * *

Anne stood in the middle of the room, facing the door. How could she do this? How could she plan to shoot another person? It was against all she had ever thought or believed. But this woman, only a young girl, really, followed her, took orders from a cartel that wanted her dead. Or at least wanted the child back. The door handle, an old iron lever, depressed and Esti, at least she assumed it was Esti, tried to push the door open and failed. Perhaps she would think that no one was here and go away. Perhaps Sarah would come back and tell her that Anne had taken the child and had left. Her heart pounded in her ears, her chest tightened, every breath painful.

Explosions splintered the door frame. Anne drew back into the corner, into the shadows. A figure pushed the door out of the way. Who was this? Blonde, short hair, not Esti's long black mane. But the face that turned towards her and the angry brown eyes were Esti's.

"Your hands are shaking," Esti said. "What sort of agent did they send?"

"I'm not an agent. I'm a doctor, a children's doctor." Anne braced the hand holding the weapon with the

215

other. Her aim wavered. She drew a deep breath, and held it. Her hand steadied. She watched Esti's face for a flicker, anything that would reveal that she was about to shoot. She heard her own breath rasp as she let it go. Outside, the cockerel crowed.

Esti spoke, her voice harsh in the silence. "Soon you will be a dead children's doctor. But first you will tell me where you have hidden the child." She aimed her gun at Anne's head.

Perhaps she wouldn't shoot her before she had Naomi. Perhaps she could still talk her out of this...

"No." Another explosion of sound, and a smell that Anne recognized, reminding her of Bermuda and the shots that came towards her from the dark. A bullet buried itself in the wall near her head.

"The next one goes in your knee. Even were I to let you live, you would never walk properly again. You have caused me too much trouble. Much too much trouble."

"I will shoot you."

Would she? Anne's gun wavered again and then steadied.

"No, you will not. I am coming to take the gun from you." Esti laughed, tucked her weapon into her waistband and vaulted towards Anne across the darkened room.

Squeeze both together, Daniel said. But Esti was all ready on her, twisting the hand that held the gun. Fierce pain shot from her hand to shoulder but she still held the gun.

She heard her own howl of rage. She was swearing, battering at Esti with her free hand. She caught her fingers in the yellow curls and tore at the roots. Esti drew back her arm to hit her but Anne closed her teeth on its soft underbelly, tasted copper and salt. She'd drawn blood.

Esti screamed and dropped the hand that held Anne's wrist to hit her. Anne scrambled backwards, her infected leg collapsed, she tripped over a footstool, and in falling, tightened her grip on the trigger. The sound exploded in her ears. Esti's eyes widened and her mouth opened as though to speak, but no words came and she dropped, her weight carrying Anne to the floor.

Warm blood dripped from Esti's mouth onto Anne's face, flowed down her cheek and pooled on the floor beside her. The body, heavy and warm, held her against the floor, a crushing weight on her chest. She leveraged herself against the floor, but her left hand slipped in the blood. She took a breath, two, against the weight and tried again. Esti's dead brown eyes, inches from her face, stared at her in triumph as she struggled to free herself. Now she had her right arm loose. She still held the gun. She dropped it and reached around Esti's head. She grabbed a handful of shirt and pulled. The body rolled, freeing her. She took great breaths and then bile rising in her throat threatened to drown her. Esti's legs still trapped hers. She closed her eyes for a moment. Footsteps, running, into the farmhouse and across the floor. Who? Had Sergio come with her?

CHAPTER 32

The footsteps came closer. The gun. Where was the gun? She dug under the body, found Esti's but couldn't drag it from her belt. She patted the floor, her hand closed on the barrel of her gun and she found the handle and then the trigger.

Esti's body, hauled away, released her. The gun shook in front of the face above.

"Annie, it's me. It's me. Put down the gun."

Thomas. Was he really Thomas or did she want him to be Thomas so badly she put his face on Sergio's body?

"Thomas?"

"Yes. Put down the gun."

Thomas. She held out the gun and he released it from her hand. He lifted her from the floor and for a moment she sheltered in his arms.

"Naomi. I have to get Naomi. She can't see this. She can't."

"I'll cover the body. Go."

Anne ran back to the armoire, flung open the doors and called to Naomi.

"I'm here, Dolly. I'm here."

She unlatched the back wall, scooped the child into her arms and carried her into the kitchen.

"We're going outside now," she said to Naomi, and escaped into the fresh morning air, away from the acrid smell of the gunshot and the copper of the blood. But she carried the blood smell into the farmyard with her.

"*Safta*, where is Esti?"

"She went away."

"I heard noises, like rifles."

"No more noises. We're going to take you home."

"Who is that?"

Anne's heart leaped into her throat again, and she sheltered Naomi behind her.

The face was that of a friend.

"Adam. How—"

"Tom called me." He hugged her with one arm, but raised the gun he held in the other when a battered white truck drove down the lane from the highway and parked beside Thomas's car. Anne opened the driver's door and offered Sarah a hand.

"No, thank you. When the day comes that I can't get out of the truck by myself, I'll have to move to town."

Thomas stepped out of the farmhouse.

"Who are these men?" Sarah asked.

"Thomas and Adam, my friends. Sarah, Esti's inside."

Sarah inspected her doorway before she walked into the farmhouse.

"Naomi, can you play with the chickens while I go with Sarah for a minute."

"Yes," she said.

"I'll stay with her," Adam said.

Anne followed Thomas and Sarah into the house. He had covered Esti with a blanket from the sofa. Now he drew it back enough to show her face. The dark eyes, open and lifeless, stared at Anne. She drew away and ran to the sink at the other end of the room, vomiting, heaving until only yellow bile remained. She took a glass from the shelf but dropped it from her shaking hands. It shattered on the slate floor.

Thomas came to her and sat her in a chair and brought her a cup of water, wrapping her fingers around the handle for her.

"Drink," he said. "In a moment Sarah will bring you some wine. Don't look at Esti anymore."

He knelt beside the body and asked Sarah, "What do you want to do with her?"

"I had an intruder and I shot her," she said. "Where is Anne's gun?" She disassembled the weapon, wiping each piece as she put it together again. She replaced each bullet in the magazine, placing her own fingerprints on each one.

"Anne was down when she fired?"

"I think so."

"Help me find the bullet." She searched the ceiling and then the wall opposite the body. "Above the door."

Thomas grunted, and dug the bullet out. She wiped the blood off and placed her fingerprint on one end.

"You're sure you want to take responsibility for this?"

"*Mossad* is coming and they will clean up," she said. "They'll get rid of the body and the gun and the car. My fingerprints are just in case any someone comes before they do. My prints aren't in anyone's database."

"She stopped at the cafe in Tovo san Giacomo and asked directions to your place."

"Did she? I'm sure Ricardo will forget that if the police ask him. I want you to phone a number in Israel for me. You have a secure phone?"

"Yes."

She handed him the number and said he must ask for Adina.

"When you reach her, tell her you have a message for the minister, that all is well and his dove is flying home."

"Should we wait for *Mossad*?"

"No, others may come. Drive to Marseilles, to the consulate."

"The consulate is safe?"

"It will be."

She brought Anne a tumbler of red wine and kept a gnarled hand on her shoulder while she drank.

"Now, go," she said. "Return Naomi to her family."

* * *

The black vehicle pulled into the farmyard beside Esti's car. An agent, one of the men, passed his hand over the hood.

"Cooling," he said.

The woman pointed to the splintered front door. She motioned one of the men to circle the house, drew her gun and took a position on one side of the door. The other agent took the opposite.

"Nothing," the third agent spoke into their ears.

The man pushed the door open and stepped inside.

A wizened old woman sat in an armchair behind a blanket-covered form on the floor, pointing a pistol mounted with a silencer at the woman's head.

"And you are?" she said.

"Sarah? Adina sent me. The bird is on the wing?"

"Yes, on its way home. There is a mess to clean up here."

"We'll look after it."

Sarah sat while the agents removed the body, washed the walls and the floor with bleach and wiped every surface.

"You live alone?" the woman asked.

"Yes."

"Could you spread your fingerprints around when we've gone?"

"Yes. I must show you where the child hid." She opened the armoire and released the back wall. The agent wiped down the interior and Sarah touched a few surfaces.

"We're leaving, now. Can you tell us where they are taking the child?" one of the men asked.

The female agent slanted her eyes at him and frowned.

"No."

"They must have said something?"

"Nothing."

He opened his mouth to speak again when the woman interrupted, "We're going. Thank you, Sarah."

Sarah nodded and sat, holding her pistol until they disappeared on the road to town.

CHAPTER 33

The grandfather tossed bits of bread to pigeons clustered around his feet. Today he had chosen a bench on one of the side-paths of the park. The wall with its crown of barbed wire loomed over him, but his view was of the building that housed their democracy. A woman approached him along the path.

"How are you, Jacob?"

"Well, and you?"

"Well as can be expected at my age. Are you still waiting for word?"

"No."

"And so. Have you decided how you will vote?" She leaned forward for a view of his face.

"Not yet. Not until she is safe in the arms of her mother."

"Even if she is returned soon, she will not be in Israel before the vote. Three hours, Jacob."

"Returning is not necessary." He stood up, brushed off the crumbs, and reached out his hand. She shook it but stayed sitting.

"You are not coming back in?" he said

"Not for a little while."

Before he rounded a corner, he glanced back. She was

talking on her phone. What of that? Everyone did, all the time. But he wondered.

* * *

The drive from Menton to Marseilles along the A-9 should take two hours and thirty minutes, Thomas told her, but at St. Andre et Tunnel de la Baume, traffic slowed. Black smoke poured from another vehicle in flames. Past the slowdown, they made better time and soon they entered the outskirts of Marseilles.

Anne dozed off, but awoke with a scream.

"What?"

"I was back there again, a nightmare. You didn't come."

He took her hand. "I'll always come."

She knew that, knew he would always be there for her. Could she commit to him? Here, in danger still, driving across France, she could but what about when she returned home, to her garden and her peaceful life?

"I know," she said and squeezed his fingers. "I know."

Later, she asked, "Where is Adam?"

"Behind us, about three cars. The consulate is in the office building to the right," he said. He parked and she lifted Naomi out, strapped on her backpack, gave her the donkey and took her hand as they crossed the road. Thomas spoke to the guard at the entrance and they passed through a metal detector and into the lobby of the building.

"That is the flag of Israel," Naomi said, pointing to the white banner with its blue bands and Star of David. "We have one in the school."

"This is a little piece of Israel in France. You're home, Naomi."

"They're waiting in the Consul-General's office," the receptionist said, taking them to the elevator.

Another guard met them at the elevator and took them to the office, opening the door for them.

Inside, a woman with Naomi's wild red curls and a man with weary eyes started up from chairs near a wall of windows.

Naomi took Anne's hand again.

"Naomi," the woman said, tears coursing down her cheeks.

"*Ima!*" Naomi ran across the room and hugged her mother's knees. Her father picked her up and surrounded wife and child with his arms.

Anne turned to Thomas, hiding her face in his shirt. After a few moments, the father came to them, hand outstretched.

"How can we ever thank you?"

"No need to thank us for saving a child," Anne said. She touched Naomi's curls, pushing them back from her forehead, reached down and brushed her cheek with a kiss. "Good-bye, Naomi."

"Good-bye, *Safta.*" The little arms hugged Anne's neck and then snuggled back into her father's embrace.

The guard escorted them down to the lobby and across the street to their car.

"Where now?" Thomas asked.

"Setenil. There is still the matter of the warrant, and my clothes and my tickets."

"We can replace all that."

"No, I'd like to say good-bye to Winston."

Adam loped along the sidewalk towards them.

"Do you still need me, Tom? Otherwise, I want to arrange a flight."

"Can you hang on and follow us into Spain. Sarah said others might come."

"Even though Naomi is safe?" Anne said.

"There's always you."

Anne's stomach knotted; pain took her breath away. Fifteen days. When would it be over?

"Why?"

"You're a lot of trouble, lady."

"Let's go," Adam said. "I'm right behind you."

CHAPTER 34

In his office in the Knesset, the grandfather stuffed papers into his briefcase. He hesitated and then placed a photograph of his Naomi on top. In one hour he was scheduled to speak in the Knesset. He prayed, a plea for wisdom, for relief from the burden of choosing between his granddaughter and the future of his country. The computer on his secretary's desk rang. A moment late she raced into the office.

"Come, Jacob. Come." Only news of the child could pitch her voice so high or make her use his first name.

He hurried out, knocking a pile of his papers to the floor in his rush. She ignored that too.

"They are on Skype."

And there she was, red curls tumbling around her gamin face, a stuffed toy grasped in her arms, safe in her mother's arms.

"*Saba, Saba,*" she called. "I'm here."

He said nothing but devoured her face, each detail: her eyes the color of amber, the dusting of freckles across her nose, the delicate arch of her eyebrows, her arrowhead grin.

"Are you there, *Saba?* You're not talking. Can you hear me? *Safta* Elizabeth brought me to *Ima.*"

"Yes, yes, I'm here, my darling. How are you?"

"*Ima* is here and *Abba*. *Safta* Elizabeth brought me in the car with Thomas from Sarah's house." She chattered on, talking about the donkeys and her donkey.

"See her, *Saba*. Her name is Dafna."

"She's a lovely donkey. May I talk to your *ima* now?"

His daughter's tear-streaked face filled the screen.

"We just got her back. She's fine. She's fine."

"When will you be home?"

She turned around to the men standing behind her and asked.

"We'll be on a flight in two hours. When is the vote?"

"In one hour."

"We are safe here. Make a good choice for Israel, *Abba*. We are safe."

"Let me see her again."

"Bye, bye, *Saba*," she waved from her father's arms.

"Good-bye, my love."

An hour later he stood in the Knesset and spoke for an end to the settlements, for a two-country solution and the beginning of peace.

"Three months ago," he said, "agents of an arms cartel kidnapped my granddaughter and demanded that I speak to you in favor of the settlements and against a peaceful end to the conflict between us and Palestine. For her sake, and the sake of all the children of Israel, I vote for peace."

CHAPTER 35

Colette paced her office, oblivious to the view overlooking the Rhone at its exit from Lake Geneva. She dialed again. Where was that woman? Her last contact had been the day before, on her way to the winery. Nothing but silence since.

She sat behind her elegant desk and watched sea birds soar and dive over the river. She touched up her makeup and checked the deep-red enamel on her fingernails for chips but found only their usual perfection. Freedom. Was it time?

She hesitated over the next call. The failures were mounting up: the botched assassination in Bermuda, the death of the commander in Setenil, the detection of the mole in Israel. How long before she was through? She decided to wait an hour or two longer. Perhaps Esti had trouble locating the farm.

An hour later, she rose from her chair to answer the phone.

"No, I haven't heard from her this morning."

His tongue clicked. Annoyance. Never good with him.

"The grandfather voted this afternoon, against the settlements. According to our sources, he claims his granddaughter has been returned although he did not say so publicly. If Esti found her, arrange to kill them both. Do not fail this time, Colette. I'm fond of you, but the other directors are anxious." He terminated the conversation before she could answer.

If the grandfather had voted, Esti failed and was likely dead. Sergio died on that mountain in Spain. Only she remained of those who knew about the operation and it was time for her to disappear.

She had prepared for this. She withdrew the sim cards from all her phones, and pocketed them. Soon they would rest on the bottom of the Rhone. The next two hours she would spend wiping the hard drive of the only computer with sensitive, identifying information. She checked her account in Zurich. Enough, she thought, to disappear.

How long before they sent someone? Likely he'd call again. She initiated the erasure program on the computer. Two hours and she would be free.

* * *

Winston arrived in Lyon at 3 p.m.. The imposing glass and steel of the Interpol building at 200 Quay Charles de Gaulle reflected in the muddied waters of the Rhone. Inside, he strode across the atrium with its blue and white logo—the sword and scales of justice behind a globe—set in the middle of radiating hardwood. Above, green plants cascaded from balconies fronting offices with their windows facing in. He stopped at the reception, showed his credentials—again—to the guard and took the elevator to the floor that housed Henri's office.

"Winston, how surprised I am to see you again, so soon." He held out a hand and then waved Winston to a seating area overlooking the river. Winston sat in a black leather club chair, facing the floor-to-ceiling windows with their view of the Rhone. Far below, a cargo boat, its deck loaded with crates headed for industry upriver, chugged by.

"We need to talk about the situation in Switzerland," Winston said.

"I understand that the child has been recovered?"

"Yes. And the grandfather voted. The cartel was defeated this time." Winston stood up and watched another river boat, one carrying innocent tourists on a journey through France, pass along the quiet water.

"You're not satisfied?"

"No. I've been on the trail of this bunch for ten years, and it's time we closed them down."

"How do you propose—"

"The woman who relays the orders—" Winston turned back to the room.

"We were close before, but when we reached her office the bird had flown. Sit, sit."

"They may not know as yet that Esti failed. *Mossad* cleaned up?" He took a seat in a black leather and steel chair across from Henri.

"Yes."

"They kept her cell phone."

"They don't share." Henri crossed one elegant leg over the other and folded his arms.

"This time they owe us a favor." Winston prowled the room again.

"Sit. You're making my neck ache following you around. The mole."

"Is there anyone you're sure of?"

"Possibly. We can but try."

"Who?" Winston sat and leaned forward, waiting.

After a long moment, Henri said, "Her name is Adina."

"Make the call. Let's clear out this nest of vipers, but there's not much time."

Winston held his gaze on his old friend. Henri tapped his fingers on the arm of his chair, hesitated and then walked to his desk, and picked up a phone from a row of possibilities lined up on the top. He dialed, spoke briefly and waited.

* * *

The sun was low in the sky by the time Anne and Thomas left the consulate. Adam waited for them by his vehicle.

"So? Did it go well?"

"Very well. Will you follow us back to Setenil, or do you want to get on a plane home?"

"I'll follow you."

Thomas and Anne settled into their car for the long drive.

"Have you ever been to Marseille?" Thomas asked.

"Never."

"We should stay the night." He twisted in his seat and laid his hand on her shoulder.

She gazed out at the street across from the Consulate. Were the figures standing in a doorway lovers or agents waiting for her? She shivered and pulled the sweater Sarah gave her tighter around her shoulders. Would she never be free?

"Sergio told me that Esti forced the Guardia commander to issue a warrant for my arrest."

"What do you want to do?"

"Drive, I think, further into France, to somewhere closer to Spain. As long as you're not too tired, let's keep moving. They can't find us when we're moving." Her voice broke and she sobbed. Thomas put his arm around her and drew her towards him.

"I'll keep you safe, Anne."

He moved the car out into the traffic and headed out of Marseille.

Five hours later, he stopped at a service center for gas. Anne woke up, shaking out one nerveless hand.

"Where are we?"

"Narbonne."

Thomas went inside for bottles of water and chocolate bars. They both needed some energy. On his way out, he noticed a vehicle parked on the far side of the lot, its engine turned off and the occupants sitting.

"Anne, we may have company."

"Where, who?"

"That Ford to the right and three spots down."

"Police?" She twisted around, watching behind.

"I don't think so. We'll get back on the AutoRoute and see if they follow."

A few kilometers later, he glanced in the mirror again. The innocuous beige vehicle kept pace in the lane behind them.

"Call Adam."

Anne spoke into the phone. "There's a car following us."

"Yeah," Adam said. "I'll get behind them."

CHAPTER 36

In Lyon, Winston waited until Henri's conversation with the Israeli ended.

"And so?" he said.

"The woman, Esti, recorded all her calls, including those with the woman in Switzerland. No names but they know where she is. They suspect the cartel is sending someone for her. The young man, Esti's accomplice, died in a traffic accident in Spain."

"Convenient."

"Yes."

"We have eyes on her office building and a team going in. Would you like to come with me?"

"Of course."

A few minutes later they stood before a three-metre-wide monitor, watching a team of armed agents in helmets and body armor enter the back of an office building on a quiet street in Geneva. They and a technician were alone in the room.

"The main entrance overlooks the river," Henri said.

"How pleasant. Do any of the companies in question keep offices here?"

"None. Her office is registered to an accounting firm but she is the only occupant."

The helmet camera of the lead agent revealed an elevator. He swung his head around and directed two men up the stairs. The remaining three entered the elevator with him.

On the penthouse floor the door to the only office stood ajar.

"She's gone," Winston said. "Bloody hell." Again. After all this time.

"Or dead."

If Colette were dead, her body had been removed and the office cleaned. Only an elegant 18th century desk facing the view, a modern ergonomically-correct chair and a gooseneck lamp remained.

"Do you know who she is?"

"Not precisely. I'm sorry, Winston. We will find her."

"Is she Swiss?"

"We think so."

"She'll need cash. A woman like her would have accounts in where?" Winston asked, turning away from the monitor. They returned to Henri's office before he answered.

"Zurich." He leaned back and closed his eyes.

"Watch the banks." Winston sat opposite in one of the steel chairs, shifting his weight on the black leather seats.

"All of them?"

"Yes, all of them. It's the only way." Why doesn't he open his damn eyes?

"Tremendous use of resources."

"Cameras, live feed, how hard can it be?"

"All right. I'll ask what can be done."

Henri phoned again, this time a protracted conversation in German.

"Well?"

"It may take some time. Would you care for lunch?"

"No, I want to get back to Setenil. Thank you for your help, Henri. Please tell me if you find a trace of her." It wasn't his problem any more and he wanted to talk to Anne before she left Spain.

CHAPTER 37

Day Sixteen

Thomas drove on. The AutoRoute bisected the *Parc National* at Narbonne, first bordering the extensive lagoons and then the square salt flats, barely visible in the early morning light, encrusted white, like handkerchiefs laid out to dry in the sun.

"Have you ever been here?" Thomas asked.

"To pass, going the other way."

"Narbonne is a lovely little city, complete with a canal to the lagoon."

"Like Venice."

"Somewhat. Half the plant species of France are found here, and fifty different ecosystems with an amazing variety of fauna."

"You know a lot about it."

"For a time I lived in Montpellier and coming out to Narbonne was an escape from the routine of my job."

"What did you do in the park?"

"Birding, hiking."

Should she ask him now? Which job? His business or his CIA "ops?"

The flats gave way to low hills on one side and fields, lying fallow for the season, on the other. In another fifteen kilometers, the highway swung close to the sea. A Mediterranean scent—burning olive branches, salt, and lavender—drifted into the car. Anne took a deep, calming breath. She grew lavender at home, and for a moment she was enclosed in her garden, safe.

"This is called *Etang de Leucate*," he said.

"*Etang*? Does that mean bay or harbor?"

"More like a pond."

"We should talk."

"Do you want to stop before Perpignan?"

"Perhaps it would be easier in the car."

"Not for me."

"In Perpignan, then." What was she going to ask him? What did she want him to say to her? He couldn't change who he was, and she couldn't change what she had done.

* * *

At Perpignan, Thomas took the off-ramp for the D-900 and soon after a road down to water.

"Where are we?"

"*Lac de Villeneuve de la Raho.*"

He called Adam to tell him they were taking a short break to walk and talk. Adam parked and stood outside his vehicle, watching.

The wide blue lake expanded in front of them. Beyond shone a snow-capped mountain-top. They strolled along a narrow causeway, its surface pebbled with white stones, the water on either side reflecting the orange and purple sunrise.

"In the summer, poppies grow along the border of the causeway," he said.

Poppies, thriving in disturbed earth, beauty where

there had been only carnage: something every Canadian schoolchild learned in a November lesson.

"Thomas, how will I get over this?"

"Which this? My being CIA or Esti's death?" They reached the end of the causeway and sat on a bench as the sky faded to deep blue.

"I understand why you didn't tell me. I know your work was, is dangerous. I need to understand if you are still working for them, if I have to worry every day that you are somewhere, in Afghanistan or Russia or some other godforsaken place, risking your life, that you may not come back to me." She sought his eyes, wanting to see truth in their black depths.

"I retired from that after Bermuda. I asked Quin for a favor, to get me the information I needed to help you, and he may call it in. No pay check from the government, no ops. From now on, I'm a businessman and I may retire." He bent forward, reached for a pebble and arched it towards the water. One, two, five skips.

She curled her arm through his and leaned against his shoulder. Did she need more than this assurance? What more could he say or do? All she could do was trust.

"Esti?" she said.

"For me, her death isn't a problem, it's a solution. But when a life goes, even a life like hers, and it's your fault, the sights and sounds and smells of that moment keep returning, for a long time. All I can do is be here for you."

"So I'm broken."

"For a while. I'll help you mend."

They walked back to the car, its red surface gleaming in the early morning sunlight.

Would she ever be mended, whole again? She tightened her grip on Thomas's hand.

"Why are you limping," he said.

"My leg's infected. I have antibiotic for it."

When they left the parking lot, the beige vehicle followed. Adam pulled in behind and the parade of three drove on to Setenil.

* * *

Thomas reached Barcelona by noon, drove on to the small seaside town of Castelldefels and took an off ramp that led to a strip of hotels along the beach. Anne woke from a nap when he stopped.

"I'm done," he said. "We have to catch a few hours sleep."

"The hotel, my passport?" Her words caught in her throat and she coughed to clear them.

"It's a resort town so the clerks aren't likely to be too particular. We've passed lots of patrol cars, and no one seemed interested in us."

"It's not us. It's me. The warrant. If they scoop me up, will they listen to you?"

"Because I'm a bad-ass CIA agent?"

"Because you're a blameless businessman." Anne giggled. The giggle turned into a splutter of laughter that changed to sobs.

Thomas took her hand and waited.

"I'm sorry," she said. "I'm tired too. Let's find a hotel and rest for a little while."

"Or a day. The beach is lovely here."

An app on Thomas's cellphone found them a room in a low-rise hotel with a view of the beach and the sea. No one questioned Anne's passport. Adam walked in behind them and took a room on the same floor.

Thomas carried his bag and left the porter standing bereft beside his moveable rack. The door opened to a room, euro-chic, no softness anywhere but on the wide bed with its stacks of decorative lime-green pillows.

Anne showered and wrapped herself in the white bathrobe the hotel provided. Her leg looked better, the redness not so extensive and the pain less. She injected a dose of antibiotic.

Thomas was all ready asleep, folded into a crescent towards the side of the bed she used to choose. She lay down, softly, not wanting to wake him. After a moment, he curled around her. She stiffened and then relaxed into his arms.

A few minutes later, they both slept. Out on the road, the followers parked near Thomas's car.

* * *

Winston took his afternoon walk to the terrace and sat with his face toward the setting sun. The waiter bustled up.

"Welcome back, Senor."

"Thanks very much. Anything new here?"

The waiter glanced towards the cafe. His words tripped over themselves in his hurry to get out all the news before his boss noticed he was talking.

"Oh yes. Many things. Neither the child nor the doctor returned. The Commandant was murdered and they say that Esti did it. She has gone. Sergio disappeared and so did your new friend, the American."

"Who is investigating the deaths and so on?"

"That is what is so strange. No one has been here to ask questions or search. It is as if the police all ready know what happened."

"Even the child?"

"Yes, even her." He rushed away when his boss appeared in the cafe door.

Winston noted the tourists: the Americans sipping ten euro Cokes in the corner, the Irish drinking beer by the entrance to the cafe, the Germans—beer again—in a noisy group along the wall. No children on the terrace today. Perhaps the parents heard about Naomi's disappearance.

The plaza felt empty in spite of all the activity. He missed Anne, her blond curls streaked with grey, her green eyes asking questions, her persistence, her outrage. He shouldn't get attached to some random woman, a tourist, but he had. Where was she? If she'd left France after returning the child, would she come back here or leave without a word? He swirled the red wine in his glass and thought about the woman Anne was.

She would return and he would wait until she did.

* * *

In the late afternoon, Anne woke, startled out of sleep by a dream of a menacing horror, and screamed. Thomas jerked awake.

"What?"

"Nothing, a nightmare." His arms encircled her and he pulled her back down to the bed.

"What?"

"Something, menacing me. I dream. Sometimes I scream. It happens fairly often."

"We need to go. Your leg?"

"Better. Shall we walk on the beach for a few minutes before we leave?"

They left the car in a parking lot and wandered along beside the sea for half an hour. The Mediterranean stretched before them, lapping the pink of the sand with gentle waves, tipped gold by the setting sun.

"How peaceful," she said.

"Perhaps we'll come back one day."

"Perhaps."

Adam waited beside his car.

"On to Setenil?" he said.

Thomas nodded and Adam swung into the driver's seat.

By 8 p.m. they were on the road again.

"Find out how many hours to Setenil."

A moment with the GPS and she told him, "Nine hours, give or take. Can you drive that far in one go?"

"Yes."

"Will you avoid the mountains, as long as you can."

"We'll go by Murcia. Can you watch in your mirror for a while? We still have the tail, I think."

"The cartel?"

"Yes, or *Mossad*, making sure we get back to Setenil, or the agency."

"So menacers or minders?"

"Yes."

The beige vehicle appeared in her mirror, hanging back but matching their speed.

"There they are. What should we do?"

"Nothing as long as they're in sight and no one joins them up ahead."

Anne's phone shattered the silence with a text from Adam.

"Adam says he's behind the beige car and do you want him to stay there or get between us and it."

"Stay where he is."

How calm he was, so sure of his abilities. Anne's heart raced and she shivered. Thomas took her hand.

"You're freezing."

"Frightened. When will this be over? I thought when we returned Naomi, that would be it, but no, here we are again."

He squeezed her hand once and gripped the wheel.

"We could drive into a service center and when they park, I could demand an explanation."

"How safe is that?"

"Not."

"Then drive."

"Annie, there's a gun in the glove box. The one I took from you at the farm. It's loaded. If anything happens to me—"

"No, I won't let anything happen to you."

"Do you remember how to use it?"

"Yes. The safety's in the trigger, pull back and fire. Aim for the body mass." Vomit rose in her throat. Esti's dead eyes stared at her. She swallowed and gulped air.

"What?"

"The farm, again."

"My fault. I'm sorry."

"I'll remember what to do. I can't lose you again, Thomas. I can't."

His mouth curved into a smile and he patted her knee.

"They're still coming," she said.

"Adam's behind us and now we know."

Chapter 38

Day Seventeen

The night wore on. By 4 a.m. they passed Ronda and turned off the highway at Acinipo. Across a field the remains of a Roman theatre loomed in the headlights and disappeared.

"Did you visit the Roman ruins here," Thomas asked.

"No. I haven't been in Spain long enough to visit anything except the Reina Sophia Museum in Madrid and the Prado."

"You went to the Reina Sophia? I didn't think modern art would be to your taste."

"I wanted to see Guernica, Picasso's painting about the German attack on a village the government claimed harbored terrorists— target practice for the Germans and their new planes."

"A disturbing painting."

"It reflects my feelings about guns and violence, Thomas. And now what have I done?"

"Saved a child. Being against guns and violence doesn't mean you have to be a complete pacifist and not defend the helpless. You aren't that way. You stand up for yourself and other people too."

"When will the nightmares end?"

"Eventually. It took about six months for me, the first time I shot someone who wanted to kill me. And be sure, there was no talking Esti out of killing you and Naomi."

"Let's look at Acinipo in the moonlight," Thomas said.

"For a moment."

They parked, but before they could get out, Thomas said, "Stay inside, Anne. Someone followed us in."

"Not Adam?" Anne's heart thudded as she twisted around to see. Behind sat a black SUV, two men in the front.

Adam rolled into the entrance, lights out and stopped.

The men behind stood between the doors of their vehicles and called to them to get out of the car.

"We want the woman. Give her to us and we'll let you live."

"Oh sure," muttered Thomas. He reached across Anne and took a gun from the glove box and gave it to her.

"Remember what to do?"

"Yes."

"Will you?"

"Yes. I can't lose you again; I can't." How long will they wait for an answer before they open fire? Her chest, her throat contracted and she couldn't breathe.

Thomas opened his door and stood. Movement off to the left behind the two men. Adam, Adam was coming, she thought.

"Hell, no. Turn your vehicle around and leave and we'll not follow," Thomas shouted.

Adam fired a shot up, into the night sky.

The men dove back in, revved the engine and aimed it at Thomas. He fired at the windshield. The SUV swerved and turned back to the entrance. Two men with long weapons waited for them.

"Thomas, who?"

"I don't know."

The men stopped and came out of the vehicle with their arms up. The waiting men pushed them to their knees and handcuffed them.

The agents. If that's who they were, held their arms away from their bodies as they walked towards Thomas and Anne.

"And you are?" Thomas said in a voice colder than Anne had ever heard before.

"Interpol. Our boss ordered us to mind you." One of them held out credentials.

"Did that include following us without advising us of who you are? Anne's not an agent; you frightened and upset her."

The lead man, older, with some grey in his dark hair, held out his hand to Anne. His American accent surprised her.

"My apologies but we had information that the cartel had sent others after you. We also wanted to tell you the warrant issued for you was vacated. The commandant is dead. The woman, Esti, killed him."

Anne covered her face with her hands to hide the sudden tears. A weight fell from her chest and she could breathe again. After a moment she clasped the agent's hand.

"Thank you," she said. "Are we safe now? The cartel…"

"We raided the headquarters but we found no sign of the woman who relays the cartel's orders. I expect she's history. Too many failures. They'll need time to regroup and we might get them. We're still hunting for her and if we find her, we may learn enough to put them all away.

"These men?"

"Hired. They won't know who gave the orders."

So not safe, but safer.

"How did Interpol get involved with this, with us?" Thomas asked.

"Someone here, I think, contacted our boss."

The minders drove off, and Anne and Thomas returned to their car. Adam loped up to the window.

"What now, Tom."

"On to Setenil."

* * *

They approached the village from across the river. The whitewashed houses, in tiers on and in the rock, shone in the moonlight.

"Odd. I feel as though I'm coming home," Anne said.

"Familiarity."

Adam walked with them through the tunnel of rock to Anne's house.

"Tom, I'm going on tonight. I can reach Seville by morning and take the train to Madrid."

Anne hugged him. "There's a couch, Adam."

"No, I'm good. Don't be a stranger. Come visit us in Culver's Mills."

"I will."

"Someone here?" Thomas said.

"Winston was the only one who knew. I'll ask him tomorrow."

Anne found the key for the blue door in her pocket, amazed that she still had it after everything.

Inside, he said, "Do you want me to find somewhere else to stay? There's only one bed."

"One is all we need, isn't it."

An hour later, they slept.

* * *

Daniel sat under an orange tree, his gaze down the long rows to where his brother and Shoshana worked on a tree that needed some pruning. Two weeks ago he left message for Anne in Madrid. Two weeks ago he'd been a *Mossad* agent. And now? He relaxed back in his chair. Now he raised oranges and soon children. Anne had asked if he meant in that order, and he had said yes, but Shoshana's news changed everything. A child before the oranges. His sister-in-law called to him from the doorway to the house.

"Daniel, you have a visitor."

He struggled to get to his feet, but the visitor, an older man with grey hair, hurried to his side.

"Sit, sit," he said.

His sister-in-law brought a chair for the visitor. He sat and held out his hand.

"I'm—"

"Yes, sir."

"I came to thank you for what you did for us and for Israel."

"I was proud to help, but the Canadian, Anne McPhail, she did more than I ever imagined she could."

"You set most of that up for her. I understand you are retiring. Are your injuries so severe? I was told you would make a full recovery."

"You see the woman pruning the trees," he said, pointing down the row to Shoshana. "I promised her

I've been on my last job. Being with your grand-daughter...I want children of my own."

"Someday, Israel may need you again."

"A problem for another day, another time. I'm not young anymore, Minister. I'm worried though. About the mole."

"We apprehended her."

"Her?"

"A confidential old friend. A devastating discovery."

"Not Adina?" Daniel leaned forward. Surely not Adina.

"No, not Adina."

"Why did she do it?"

"Money, only money."

A man in a dark suit appeared in the doorway.

"We must go, Minister."

"Daniel, our thanks and our hopes for your future, from me, my family and your country."

"Tell Naomi I miss her and her donkey."

"That donkey. She won't give it up, even for a cleaning. I'll bring her to visit you one day soon."

"I would like that."

Daniel watched Shoshana stride up the row towards him. Soon there would be a child to play with Naomi when she came. Shoshana bent down to kiss him.

"Time for your walk, lazybones. Who visited you?"

"The grandfather of the little girl in Spain."

Chapter 39

Day Eighteen

Anne woke before Thomas, slipped out of bed without waking him and gathered the few of her belongings that were scattered around the villa. The last item was the glass paperweight Daniel sent her in Madrid. Memory flooded back and she was in the farmhouse again with Esti, staring at her with dead eyes. She dropped the globe and sank to the floor. The vision receded. When she looked up, Thomas was there.

"What happened?"

"Now her face intrudes on my thoughts when I'm awake. What am I going to do?"

Thomas crouched beside her and took her hands, enveloping them in his long fingers.

"You'll need some therapy for this. It will get better, but it takes some time. We'll go home—"

"Today?"

"Yes, today, if we can get to Madrid and I can get us on a flight out of here to Toronto or New York. You're a strong woman, Anne. You'll get better."

"I'll never be the same."

"None of us are the same today as we were yesterday. That's what life does, changes us day by day."

Anne retrieved her hands and stood up.

"I'm going to pack," she said and took her collection upstairs. Therapy. Where was she going to find a therapist who would understand the kind of trauma she'd been through? But what made her different from anyone—soldier, police, spy—who had killed for the first time? She'd find someone to help. Perhaps Thomas knew a therapist.

An hour later, she came down to find Thomas reading a newspaper.

"You went out?"

"To the shop around the corner. Are you ready to go?"

"Yes. I'm supposed to leave the key at that shop."

Anne's blue raincoat matched the front door of the villa. She would have to get rid off it when she got home. It would forever remind her of these two weeks and what she did. She locked the door, pausing to rest her hand against the rough boards.

"I thought I could recover here, but now..."

"Home, Anne. We need to go home."

The rain, threatening when they left the villa, arrived in torrents by the time they reached the terrace cafe. Juanito and the owner scurried to fold the umbrellas and lean the chairs against the outside tables.

Thomas dragged the baggage inside. In the front window, with a view of the terrace and the hills beyond, sat Winston, reading the Times and drinking espresso. Beyond him, deeper in the cave that formed the cafe, three other men played cards under a hanging lamp, and a woman wiped the top of the case that held the pastries and tapas. A row of bottles, reds and whites and rich chartreuse, ranged along the wall behind the bar.

"I'm going to take these to the car," Thomas said, and hurried out into the rain.

Anne sat across from Winston and reached for his hand. "Thank you," she said.

"You're leaving too?"

"Yes."

"Must you? I shall miss you. This is a good place in which to recover from whatever happened to you."

"It didn't go well, Winston. Esti is dead. I had a gun and she fought with me to get it and I pulled the trigger. If I hadn't, in a moment Thomas would have been there." Her eyes filled and she sought his for reassurance or understanding.

"So it's okay for Thomas to kill someone who wants to kill you but not okay for you?" He sounded so angry. Why?

"But he's… No, of course not." She averted her eyes. How cowardly he must think her.

"You have been…stalwart. You saved the child when I didn't even believe she was in danger. Remember Naomi."

"Naomi."

"Yes, Naomi."

His hands, manicured but rough still, caressed hers.

"Are you committed to Thomas?" he asked.

Anne withdrew her hands, gave his a gentle pat and said, "I think I am, Winston. I have to process everything, but I think so."

"You can always find me here."

"Even if you're away on one of your photo shoots?"

"I'll come back." He passed a card across the table. "Let me know how you get on."

"I will." She stood up. He kissed her on each cheek and held her in a brief embrace. His heart thudded through his shirt.

Thomas came through the door at that moment. She pulled away from Winston, who held out his hand to Thomas.

"Thank you," Thomas said.

"Safe journey."

CHAPTER 40

In Seville, they left the car at the airport and took the AVE, the fast train to Madrid. Anne slept, and Thomas worked on a proposal for his company, neglected for the past week. An e-mail from his mother suggested he remember to call her, demanded to know what had happened to Anne. Had it been only a week since Anne's call for help?

He replied that all was well and they'd be home soon. Anne snuggled into her seat, and dropped her head onto his shoulder. He hoped all was well. What happened when she spoke to Winston? The man loved her. What were her feelings for Winston, for him? Had he lost her? On the journey back to Setenil, he thought her old feelings for him returned, but now? He leaned back in his seat and watched the countryside whip by. Soon he slept.

Three hours later they arrived in Madrid. Before they left the station, Anne took him to see the arboretum that grew under the dome and the turtles, safe in their watery home beneath a camouflage of green plants.

Anne waited outside the Arrivals hall at the airport, by the statue—a twisted, smooth mass of bronze, a female figure lounging on a bull, called *El Rapto de Europa*—the Kidnapping of Europa by Columbian artist

Fernando Botero Angulo—that had welcomed her to Spain, while Thomas arranged tickets home. She ran her hand over its polished surface. The morning sun played over the statue, surrounding her with light and warmth.

After a time Thomas stepped through the doorway, searching the courtyard for her. His face lit up when he saw her and her heart leaped.

"Success?"

"Yes, two in first class, leaving in four hours. We have to hurry to check the bags."

They hustled through the airport, checked their bags and waited in the first class lounge, relaxing in deep brown leather chairs, drinking tiny perfect cups of espresso and reading the latest news from the rest of the world. Israel had released prisoners to help with the peace negotiations but soon after had announced further expansion of the settlements.

"Did you read this?" Anne said, indicating the article.

"Yes."

"What was it all for? They voted the way the cartel wanted in spite of Naomi's grandfather. Deaths—the commander, Sergio, Esti—and Daniel wounded. Naomi may never forget the uncertainty of those sixteen days. Meaningless, all of it."

"We did what we could. We saved Naomi and took her and her donkey home. Concentrate on her." He reached for her hand and held it while she wept.

When the flight was called, they boarded and settled into the cocoons first class seats had become with modern redesign.

Anne relaxed back in her seat. Eighteen days since she arrived in Spain. Eighteen days and her life was turned around. Again. It had been about trust—trust in Thomas, trust in Sarah, even trust in Sergio but most of all trust in herself.

The steward offered Prosecco.

"What shall we toast to?" Thomas asked.

She paused, searching for the words to express her feelings. "To Naomi's safe return and to journeys that end in lovers meeting."

A delighted smile animated his face and his dark eyes sought hers.

"To Naomi and our journey's beginning."

The End

ABOUT VIRGINIA WINTERS

Virginia Winters was born in Arnprior, Ontario, Canada and raised in the Ottawa Valley. After high school in Renfrew, another Valley town, she went down to Queens to study medicine, graduating in 1970. Fellowship in Pediatrics followed, with graduation in 1976. That year she and her husband, Internist George Winters, moved to Lindsay, Ontario with their two children, and have lived there ever since. Virginia's interests, besides writing, are genealogy, gardening, photography, and studying languages (currently Spanish). *The Facepainter Murders* is the second in the *Dangerous Journeys* series.

Murderous Roots, Virginia Winters's first novel, an e-book, was published on December 1, 2009 by Write

Words Inc. and is now available in paper from that press and at Amazon.com.

Short works have appeared online in *Camroc Press Review, Six Sentences,* and *Pine Tree Mysteries* and most recently in the *Gumshoe Review.* Short stories have been published in *Confabulation 2* and *3,* anthologies produced by Wynterblue Publishing, North Bay, Ontario.

Virginia blogs about writing and other interests, including genealogy, current events and gardening at her web site:

http://www.virginiawinters.ca.

She also posts book reviews, and some of her photography. Her blog is also available at:

http://ginny200.wordpress.com/